GRADUATION SUMMER

We Can't Wait

By Emma Harrison

📖 HarperEntertainment
An Imprint of HarperCollins*Publishers*

A PARACHUTE PRESS BOOK

A PARACHUTE PRESS BOOK

Parachute Publishing, L.L.C.
156 Fifth Avenue
New York, NY 10010

Published by
HarperEntertainment
An Imprint of HarperCollins*Publishers*
10 East 53rd Street, New York, NY 10022-5299

GRADUATION SUMMER books are created and produced by Parachute Publishing, L.L.C., in cooperation with Dualstar Publications, a division of Dualstar Entertainment Group, LLC., published by HarperEntertainment, an imprint of HarperCollins Publishers.

ISBN 0-06-072282-7

HarperCollins®, ■®, and HarperEntertainment™ are trademarks of HarperCollins Publishers Inc.

First printing: July 2004

Printed in the United States of America

Visit HarperEntertainment on the World Wide Web at
www.harpercollins.com

10 9 8 7 6 5 4 3 2 1

CHAPTER ONE

Sweet freedom!" Mary-Kate Olsen called out at the top of her lungs. A cheer went up from the crowd around her, and she laughed, loving the light-as-air-feeling in her heart.

Mary-Kate was perched on the roll bar of her friend Trevor Reynolds's new Jeep Wrangler, surveying the massive party. The entire senior class of Ocean View High had gathered at the beach on this last Friday before finals, parking their cars right up against the sand and bringing drinks, snacks, and CDs to help party the night away. A bonfire roared, and music blared from a boom box as people laughed, chatted, and danced. It was a let-off-steam-before-finals-week thing—a yearly Ocean View senior class tradition.

"We're not free yet. We still have to get through the fund-raising auction, the senior awards banquet, senior cut day, graduation practice, *and* finals," her friend Claudia Pierce said from her perch next to Mary-Kate.

"Yes, but most of that stuff is fun. And Ocean View senior finals are notoriously easy," Ashley said, looking up at them from the sand. "And after this week we'll never have to take another high school test!"

"I don't believe you," Ashley's best friend, Felicity Lopez, teased, wrapping a slim arm around Ashley's shoulders. "I figured you'd *miss* taking tests."

"Won't you go through withdrawal?" Claudia asked.

"Come on, you guys! It's not like Ashley studies *all* the time," Mary-Kate said, jumping down to the sand.

"Yeah! Remember that three-hour break I took back in February?" Ashley joked.

"I think it's cool that Ashley is our valedictorian," Trevor put in, coming around the side of the Jeep with a soda cup. He was trailed by Cooper Firenz, Claudia's longtime boyfriend, who had been checking out the four-wheel-drive's off-road tires.

"Me, too," Cooper added. "I say we raise a toast to Ashley Olsen, Ocean View High's number one brain!"

Claudia jumped down, and the six friends raised their cups. "To the number one brain!" they all cheered, clicking plastic against plastic.

Kids around them laughed, and Mary-Kate saw her sister flush. Ashley was often teased for being a brainiac, but Mary-Kate was proud of her sister's accomplishments, and she knew Ashley was, too.

"Now that school is almost over, I think it's about time I kick this study-aholic image, don't you, guys?" Ashley asked, tossing her long, dark blond hair over her shoulders.

"Interesting," Felicity said, narrowing her eyes. "What did you have in mind?"

"I want to do something crazy," Ashley said. "Something I've never done before. Maybe a few things I've never done before. And I think we all should."

Mary-Kate grinned at her sister. "We should all do something *you've* never done before?"

"Ha-ha," Ashley said, rolling her eyes. "No! I'm sure there's something each of us has always wanted to do, but has never had the guts for. I say we each promise to do one crazy thing within the next two weeks."

"Like a senior-year resolution," Mary-Kate said with a thrill of excitement. That sounded like a good idea to her. She smiled at Trevor, and he grinned back at her, his deep brown eyes crinkling at the corners. Mary-Kate's heart thumped extra-hard. Trevor was her best friend. He knew her better than almost anyone did, so they were always sharing private smiles. What he didn't know was that those private smiles sent her heart into a total spasm.

If I had a senior year resolution, I know exactly what it would be, Mary-Kate thought. *I'd ask Trevor out.*

"What? Why are you looking at me like that?" Trevor asked, bringing one hand to his nose. "Is there something on my face?"

Mary-Kate blinked and blushed. "Nah. Just stunned as always by your hideousness," she joked.

"Whatever, *troll.*" He bumped her with one shoulder.

3

"Ogre," she replied, giggling and shoving him back.

Trevor tickled her, and Mary-Kate screeched and ran. He chased her around the back of the Jeep, his bare feet kicking up sand. Trevor's feet were bare whenever possible. He was always slipping off his shoes in class and sometimes walked the halls in socks or even without them. He said shoes constricted his creativity. How he'd come to that conclusion, Mary-Kate didn't know.

"There's no point in running. I always catch you," Trevor called out.

"I'd like to see you try!" Mary-Kate took off again, but within seconds Trevor grabbed her around the waist. Mary-Kate shouted and struggled. Her heart pounded as he picked her up, carried her back to the group, and deposited her on the sand. She lost her balance and stumbled into him. His lips were right there. . . .

Kiss him! Just kiss him! she thought, for a moment believing she could actually do it. *What's the worst that could happen?*

Well, he could push me away and laugh until he fainted, she realized with dread.

"You guys are like one of those coyote-roadrunner cartoons," Ashley said.

"Except the coyote never catches the roadrunner," Trevor said, running a hand over his choppy brown hair. "I always get *my* bird."

This is pathetic. He calls me his bird and I get butterflies, Mary-Kate thought. *I've got it* bad *!*

"Hello? Can we get back to the topic here?" Felicity said as she tied her long dark hair up into a ponytail. "I know what my resolution is. I am going to pull the biggest senior prank in Ocean View High history. I'm going to be *infamous*!"

"Like you aren't already," Ashley said.

Felicity was always cutting up and getting sent to the office for arguing with teachers or playing tricks. This prank idea was definitely right up her alley.

"I think I'll dye my hair red before the prom," Claudia said, pulling a strand of her chin-length blond hair in front of her eyes. "I've always wanted to try something different."

"Red, huh?" Cooper said, wrapping an arm around her. "That would be cool. Maybe *I'll* go blond."

Claudia mussed his curls, then the couple smiled and touched foreheads in their ridiculously cute way.

"My resolution is to get out there and live life to the fullest," Ashley said. "It's time for a whole new Ashley. One who takes chances."

"Kind of vague, no?" Mary-Kate said, trying to focus on the conversation and not on Trevor. She wished she could be all mushy with him the way Claudia and Cooper were. Her heart ached for it.

"Well, I've got a few things in mind. Like first, I think it's time for me to start doing some actual dating," Ashley said. "I've been so busy studying for four years, I've never had time to play the field."

"Fixing on anyone in particular?" Mary-Kate asked, glancing at Trevor.

"Well, I've always thought Todd Parker was cute," Ashley said, looking across the sand at Todd and his friends around the bonfire.

"And he just broke up with Kylie, so it's perfect timing," Claudia put in.

"Exactly," Ashley said. "Then there's David, Hunter, Scott, Joe—"

"Hey! Leave some for the rest of us!" Felicity exclaimed.

"What else is involved in 'the whole new Ashley'?" Claudia asked.

"I'll keep you posted," Ashley replied mysteriously.

"What about you, Trevor?" Mary-Kate asked. "What's your end-of-senior-year resolution?"

Trevor pressed his lips together in thought. "I think I should finally go to a school dance. Even though I am far too cool for them," he joked.

"Well, there's only one left. The prom," Mary-Kate told him.

"Exactly," Trevor said.

Suddenly a new dread came over Mary-Kate. If Trevor was going to the prom, who would be his date? Would she have to watch him dance with some other girl all night long?

Trevor placed his cup on the hood of the Jeep, got down onto one knee, and took both of Mary-Kate's hands in his. "Mary-Kate Olsen, will you do me the honor of being my date for this most important of shindigs?" he asked, eyebrows raised dramatically.

Everyone laughed, even Mary-Kate, but inside her pulse was pounding. If only he weren't kidding around!

"Sure," she told him as if it was no big deal. "Why not? We can go as friends, right?"

"Did I hear someone talking about the prom?" a new voice cut in.

Trevor stood up quickly and moved a little closer to Mary-Kate as if he was seeking protection. Hovering not five feet away was Kristi Carlton, the superannoying cheerleading-squad captain who had been practically stalking Trevor all year. She was superficial, obnoxious, and always surrounded by at least three friends from the squad—as she was now. Mary-Kate knew that the girl called Trevor almost every night, even after he'd told her straight out he wasn't interested.

"I don't have a date yet, Trevor," she said, sauntering over to him. She twirled a few strands of her shiny brown hair around one index finger.

"Oh, Kristi! You're too late!" Mary-Kate said, looping her arm through Trevor's. "He just asked *me.*"

"You two are going together?" Kristi asked, shocked. "I thought she was like a *sister* to you," she said, looking at Trevor. Kristi's friends laughed.

Did he tell her that? Mary-Kate wondered, her heart falling. *Is that what he really thinks?*

"Well, you thought wrong," Trevor said, tightening his grip on Mary-Kate and sending a skitter of excitement up her arm.

"Well, have fun then," Kristi said. "If that's possible."

Mary-Kate's mouth opened, but she couldn't think of a single comeback. She watched Kristi leave, knowing she would come up with the perfect retort in half an hour. But she forgot all about Kristi when Trevor hugged her.

"You saved me!" he announced as the others laughed. "How can I ever repay you?"

"What're friends for?" Mary-Kate said, flushing.

"So, what crazy thing are *you* going to do?" Trevor asked as he let her go.

Already Mary-Kate wished she was back in his arms. "Oh . . . I don't know," she said. It wasn't as if she could tell him her resolution in front of everyone. "I was thinking I'd start a new tradition at Ocean View. Something to make sure our class is always remembered."

As senior class president, making up a new tradition was something Mary-Kate had considered doing anyway. But now she would definitely have to.

"Sure that's not *too* crazy?" Ashley teased.

Mary-Kate laughed good-naturedly. If only Ashley knew what she was really thinking, then she'd realize how daring Mary-Kate was going to be. By asking Trevor out, she would risk losing a friendship that had been tight since the sixth grade, and she definitely didn't want that to happen.

But this was her last chance. In the fall she was going away to school on the East Coast, and she might never see Trevor again. If she ever wanted him to be her boyfriend, she had to do something. Now.

"So, Ashley, who's it going to be first?" Felicity asked.

"Todd Parker, definitely," Ashley said, watching him as he laughed with his friends by the fire. Her pulse raced at the thought of approaching him. Todd wasn't all that tall, but he was broad and strong thanks to his star status on the football field. He had blond hair, cute freckles, and all kinds of muscles. "I've had a crush on him forever, but he's always been with Kylie."

"Until now," Mary-Kate said. "So go for it."

"You mean *now* now?" Ashley asked, her stomach turning.

"No, later now," Mary-Kate joked. "Yes, now!"

"Yeah, Ash! Isn't that the whole point? To get out there and live life?" Felicity prodded.

Ashley felt a little rush. She could do this. Right?

"You're right," she said with a nod. "*Carpe Diem!*"

"Huh?" Felicity said, her face screwing up in confusion. "What about carp?"

"Not *carp*. *Carpe!*" Ashley said. "*Carpe Diem* means *seize the day* in Latin. And you guys better remember that, because I'm using it in my speech for graduation."

"Ashley! School is almost over! I am not learning another language now," Cooper whined.

Ashley rolled her eyes at him, then took a deep breath. "Okay. What do I do?" she asked, grabbing her sister's hand and lowering her voice.

Felicity, Claudia, and Mary-Kate gathered around her, moving away from the guys.

"Well, he's right over there by the boom box," Mary-Kate said. "So let's go dance!"

"Yeah!" Felicity said. "First he'll see your killer moves, and then you can 'accidentally' bump into him." Felicity scrunched her fingers into air quotes when she said *accidentally*. The girl loved her air quotes.

"Perfect," Ashley said with a grin.

The girls left Cooper and Trevor behind and headed for the makeshift dance area. Ashley made her way around to the far side, near Todd, and started to dance. Of course, she had forgotten to put down her soda, so her moves weren't exactly stellar. She had to constantly make sure she wasn't spilling all over everyone.

"Ooh! He's looking over here," Claudia said, grasping Ashley's free wrist as they danced.

"He is?" Ashley said, trying not to look.

"Dance closer to him!" Mary-Kate whispered.

Ashley did as she was told, moving backward and swaying to the music, all the while balancing her drink. She inched closer to him, and closer, and closer. . . .

Time for the accidental bumping, Ashley thought.

She took one last step, and something hit her arm—and she spilled her drink all over herself. That was *not* part of the plan. Ashley saw Mary–Kate and Felicity wince in sympathy.

Still, the plan had worked. Todd reached out and grasped her arm to steady her.

"Oh . . . whoa. I'm so sorry. You okay?" he asked. "That was totally my fault." He grabbed a few napkins and handed them to her.

Yeah, right. I was the one dancing backward! Ashley thought. Her face burned with embarrassment.

"I'm fine," she said. "Nothing broken."

I'm just the klutz of the year, she added silently.

"Good!" Todd said with a smile. "Let me get you another soda."

When he returned with Ashley's new soda, she couldn't help noticing that the necklace he'd always worn when he was with Kylie was gone. Everyone knew she'd given him the chain with his football number on it as an anniversary gift. Apparently he was really over his ex.

"So, school's almost over, huh?" Ashley said, swinging her hair over her shoulders and ignoring the stain on her dress. "Any big social events planned?"

"Nah. Not really," Todd said with a shrug. "I don't even have a date for the prom."

"Really?" Ashley said, psyched. "That's surprising."

Ask him! she thought. But when she tried to open her mouth, the words seemed to choke her. She couldn't get them out. What if he said no? It would be even more humiliating than the soda stain. *Okay, Plan*

B, she thought, trying not to panic. *Get him to ask you!*

"I don't even know if I really want to go," Todd said. "It's kind of 'been there, done that,' you know?"

"Yeah . . . totally," Ashley said, disappointed. Was he kidding? Who didn't want to go to their senior prom? She had only spent half the year working on the prom committee to make sure it was the greatest night of their lives. "But I don't know. It could be cool," she said. "I don't have a date either, though. Yet."

I'm sending you a million signals, she thought. *Ask me!*

"Oh. Bummer," Todd said, taking a sip of his drink.

One of his football buddies came over and slapped his hand. While he was distracted, Ashley turned and looked at her friends, desperate.

"Ask him!" Mary-Kate mouthed. *"Ask him to do something . . . anything!"*

"So . . . Mary-Kate and I are having some people over to swim tomorrow," Ashley told Todd casually. "Do you want to come?"

Todd's face lit up, and Ashley instantly relaxed. "Yeah, cool," he said. "Thanks for inviting me."

"Okay, then. I'll see you around one?"

"Sounds good," Todd said. "See you then."

Ashley turned around and walked as slowly as possible to her friends so he wouldn't see how excited she was.

"So? What did he say?" Mary-Kate asked eagerly.

"We have to have a pool party," Ashley replied, squeezing her sister's hand. *"Tomorrow!"*

AshleyO invites Felicity_girl and Claude18 to Instant Message!

AshleyO: So are u guys coming tomorrow?

Felicity_girl: pool party! woohoo!!

AshleyO: I'll take that as a yes.

Claude18: Will be there!

AshleyO: MK and I are shopping in the
    A.M. Any requests???

Felicity_girl: NEED nachos.

Claude18: fel, u r gonna turn n2 a
    nacho!

Felicity_girl: must have nachos.

AshleyO: ooooKAY! Now which bathing
    suit will get Todd's attention--
    black or red?

Felicity_girl: red! color of LOVE!!! ;-)

Claude18: Red. Def red.

AshleyO: But I kinda like the way I
    look in the black.

Claude18: will come over early 2 help u
    decide.

Felicity_girl: YES! as long as there
    are NACHOS!!!

AshleyO: Okay, freak! Signing off! See
    u tomorrow!

CHAPTER TWO

hanks for letting us have this party at the last minute, you guys," Ashley told her parents on Saturday afternoon. Her mom and dad were helping her fill up a plastic tray with veggies and dip while the party raged in the backyard.

"No problem," her dad said with a smile, "as long as you and your sister find time to study this weekend."

"We will!" Mary-Kate told them, rushing by and grabbing a carrot stick. "Come on, Ashley. Everyone's wondering where we are."

"We'll be upstairs if anyone needs us!" their mother called after them.

Ashley followed her sister out back, marveling at the number of kids milling around the pool, splashing in the water, and munching refreshments at the table.

"Where did all these people come from?" Ashley asked as they made their way around the pool. "Didn't I just come up with this idea last night?"

"I guess everyone was looking for a chance to party,"

Mary-Kate said with a laugh. They both screeched as Trevor splashed them from the deep end. "You're so dead!" Mary-Kate shouted at him. She cannonballed off the side of the pool, thoroughly dousing him.

Ashley shook her head at her sister, then made her way to the snack table. She put down the veggies, and instantly Carlos Bernal, the class salutatorian—the number two brain—snagged a piece of celery.

"Hey, Ashley," he said, flashing his wide smile. "Great party."

"Thanks, 'los," Ashley said.

She and Carlos had most of their classes together and were always comparing grades. Up until the very end they had been neck and neck for valedictorian, and Ashley suspected that only a serious knack for chemistry had given her the edge.

"How's your graduation speech coming?" he asked.

"It's . . . coming," Ashley said. "To tell you the truth, I haven't had much time to work on it yet."

"Me neither—on mine," Carlos said. "Maybe we should get together sometime next week to go over our ideas. You know, just to make sure we don't talk about the same things."

"Good idea!" Ashley said. "And it'll give me an incentive to get to work."

"Cool. I'll give you a call," Carlos said before moving back toward his friends.

Ashley made her way to the lounge chairs where

Claudia and Felicity were sitting and plopped down on the end of Felicity's chair.

"So, where's my date?" she asked. "I told him to be here at one."

"Check it out!" Felicity said, pointing. Sure enough, Todd was coming out the back door of the house.

Wow, Ashley thought excitedly. *My date is cute!*

Todd was wearing a white polo shirt that showed off his tan and a pair of flowered board shorts. Ashley got up to greet him, but just then his ex-girlfriend, Kylie, walked out right behind him. Ashley's heart dropped as the girl slipped her hand into Todd's. He looked back and planted a quick kiss on her lips.

What's going on here? Is he bringing his ex-girlfriend on our date? Ashley thought. *Because that is unacceptable.*

She sat down again—hard. "I thought they broke up," she said, her spirits falling flat.

Todd saw her, said something to Kylie, and walked over to Ashley solo.

"Hey, Ashley! Thanks for inviting me today," Todd said. "It gave me something to invite Kylie to, and I think we may be getting back together."

What was he talking about? Hadn't he agreed to go out with *her*?

Okay, don't let him see you crushed, Ashley thought. She swallowed her pride and her shock all in one gulp.

"Uh . . . no problem," she said, noticing his necklace was back on.

"Catch ya later," Todd said.

He walked off, and Ashley looked at her friends, totally deflated.

Claudia rubbed Ashley's back in sympathy.

"'Do you want to go with *me* to a party,'" Felicity said. "The next time you have to say, 'Do you want to go with *me.*'"

"Yeah. I'll have to remember that," Ashley said, feeling awful. Her first stab at her dating resolution had crashed and burned. Big-time.

"Forget about Todd," Felicity said as Mary-Kate walked over, wrapping a towel around herself. "I still haven't come up with a prank idea."

"Felicity, I'm shocked!" Mary-Kate said, sitting on a chair next to Claudia's. "You're usually so motivated to commit wacky hijinks."

"I know, but my brain's a blank," Felicity said with a frown. "I was thinking we could plant something in the quad—something funny. But what? Should we steal Overlook High's mascot?"

"That has *so* been done," Ashley said.

"What about a statue or something? Like that one of the gold miners in the park?" Claudia said.

"Claude, can you say 'destruction of public property'?" Ashley said. "I don't know about you, but I'd rather go to college than jail."

"Good point," Claudia said.

"There has to be something. . . ." Ashley racked her

brain for an idea, thinking of all the random landmarks around town, thanks to Claudia's suggestion. There was the Burger Boy outside Burger Bob's restaurant, and the crab on top of the Crab Shack, but they couldn't take either of those without getting into serious trouble. Then suddenly it hit her.

"I've got it! Crusty the Cow!" she blurted out.

"That rusty old eyesore?" Claudia asked.

Crusty was a huge ancient metal cow that stood in front of an abandoned farm at the edge of town. The thing had been there so long that it was totally rusted over, and no one seemed to know who owned the farmland.

"Yeah! It doesn't belong to anybody and it's at that point where it's so ugly, it's chic!" Ashley said happily.

"It does have a certain vintage charm," Mary-Kate said. "I love it!"

"I'm impressed," Felicity said. "This 'whole new Ashley' thing has its benefits."

"Hey, *carpe diem*!" Ashley said, beaming. "Okay," she added, leaning in toward them. "Here's what we should do. . . ."

"Mary-Kate, this was the best fund-raising idea ever," Ashley said on Monday morning.

"I know. I'm just a huge marketing whiz," Mary-Kate joked. "I mean, who wouldn't want to buy one of the senior guys and then get to order him around all day?"

Mary-Kate and her sister walked into the cafeteria, and instantly Mary-Kate beamed with pride. It seemed like every girl in the senior class had shown up. They were seated along the stage and the catwalk that had been used for that year's school fashion show back in December. Dark blue curtains hung at the back of the stage and a bunch of senior guys milled around behind them, talking, laughing, and checking their hair in handheld mirrors.

"I hope we make a lot of cash," Mary-Kate said, nervously checking the crowd as she and Ashley stepped onto the stage. "We need a couple of hundred dollars more to pay for the class gift."

"Please! We'll make at least that!" Ashley replied, glancing back at the guys. "These guys clean up well. I mean, who knew Ricky Meyer even *owned* a shirt with a collar?"

Mary-Kate laughed. Ricky Meyer was a notorious T-shirt addict, but he did look totally cute today in a burgundy shirt and gray pants. *Maybe this idea really will pay off,* Mary-Kate thought as she stepped to the podium. Ashley stood off to the right with a notebook and pen to record the winning bids.

"Welcome, everyone, to the Ocean View High Senior Class Personal Assistant Auction!" Mary-Kate announced into the microphone. The last few stragglers took their seats, and the room buzzed with excitement. "All right, ladies, you know how this works. If you want to bid on one of the guys, don't be shy—just shout out your bids. But remember, keep it clean, people. We don't want anyone ending up in the nurse's office over a bidding war."

The girls in the audience laughed, and Felicity shot her a thumbs-up from the front row.

"We'll start the auction off with Sean Gelb, our very own Most Likely to Succeed!" Mary-Kate announced.

Sean walked up to the stage in a dark blue button-down shirt and chinos and strode down the catwalk.

"Sean is president of no fewer than six clubs here at Ocean View High—everything from the Spanish Club to the Young Entrepreneurs Society," Mary-Kate read from Sean's info card. "He's always very busy, but he wants all bidders to know that he is ready and willing to make time for *you*!" she said with a grin as Sean winked at the audience. "We'll start the bidding at ten dollars."

"Ten!" Lara Morales shouted from the back of the room.

"I have ten. Do I hear eleven?" Mary-Kate asked.

"Eleven!" Danielle Gordon called out.

"Twelve!" a third girl chimed in.

"Thirteen!" Lara shouted.

"Fifteen dollars!" Danielle shouted.

"Wow! Our first P.A. is demanding a high price," Mary-Kate said, impressed. Everyone laughed as Sean shrugged modestly. "The high bid is fifteen dollars. Anyone else? Going once, going twice . . . sold to Danielle Gordon for fifteen dollars!"

Sean stepped down and walked over to Danielle. Ashley made a note in her book. "We're going to make two hundred in no time," she whispered to Mary-Kate.

"I know!" Mary-Kate whispered back, feeling giddy. She looked at the next name on her list, then covered the mic with one hand. "Ash! One of your potential dates is next. David Ryan."

"Oooh! I didn't know he was being auctioned!" Ashley said. "This will be so much easier than *asking* him out."

Mary-Kate laughed. "Next up, David Ryan!" she announced.

David stepped up onto the stage and struck a pose, putting his hands into his pockets and raising his eyebrows like a cheesy model. A bunch of girls in the audience laughed. David had won the title of Class Clown, easily blowing the competition away.

"David says that if you choose him as your personal assistant, you are guaranteed a day of nonstop laughing," Mary-Kate read from David's info card. "Although, ladies, he warns that he does not do windows! Shall we start the bidding at ten dollars?"

Ashley immediately raised her hand.

"We have ten from Ashley Olsen," Mary-Kate announced. "Do I hear twelve?"

"Twelve!" Meredith Griffin offered from the other side of the catwalk.

"How about thirteen, ladies?" Mary-Kate asked.

"Thirteen!" Donna Trout called out.

"Fourteen!" Ashley put in.

"Anyone want to go higher?" Mary-Kate asked the crowd. "No? Going once, going twice . . . sold to Ashley Olsen for fourteen dollars!"

Ashley beamed, and David smiled at her before walking off the stage.

"Fourteen big ones, huh?" Mary-Kate whispered as the audience applauded. "You must really like him."

"I don't actually know yet," her sister responded, marking her own bid down in her notebook. "But I *do* know I'm not ready to ask someone out again!"

"Good point," Mary-Kate said. She looked down at her notes and smiled. "Next up is Trevor Reynolds."

Trevor sauntered out from behind the curtain and walked right down the catwalk, looking as confident as a runway model.

"Oooh, now this is interesting," Mary-Kate said, grinning. "Trevor says that he'll make a perfect personal assistant because quote, 'I'll try anything once.'"

Everyone laughed, and Trevor raised his hands before executing a spin at the end of the catwalk.

"Do I hear ten dollars, ladies?"

"I'll give you twenty!" Kristi Carlton called out from the back of the cafeteria.

Mary-Kate's heart plummeted, Trevor's face went slack, and everyone turned to gape at the girl.

"Oookay," Mary-Kate said, her pulse pounding. She looked at Trevor, who stared back at her with wide eyes. Someone had to save him, but what was Mary-Kate supposed to do? She was running the show. Could she bid as well? "Do I hear . . . uh . . . twenty-five?"

Mary-Kate stared at Felicity, trying to get her to bid on Trevor. *"I'm broke!"* Felicity mouthed.

Trevor saw her and groaned audibly. He was toast.

Mary-Kate's heart pounded. She couldn't let Kristi have Trevor for a day. It would be torture for him.

"Okay, I'm going to bid twenty-five!" she said into the microphone. Trevor smiled in relief.

"Uh, can you even *do* that?" Kristi asked, hands on hips.

"Hey, money's money, right?" Mary-Kate said. "My sister, Ashley, will take over as auctioneer while I bid."

Clearly taken by surprise, Ashley tripped toward the podium. "Uh . . . is there a higher bid than twenty-five?" she asked.

"Thirty!" Kristi shouted.

"Thirty-five!" Mary-Kate put in, mentally reviewing the state of her wallet.

"Thirty-eight!" Kristi said as she scrounged in her purse.

"Forty?" Mary-Kate called out, starting to feel ill. So much for that graduation present she planned to buy Ashley.

"Uh . . . uh . . . forty-one!" Kristi shouted, all red in the face as she pulled crumpled bills from her bag.

"Forty-two!" Mary-Kate replied.

"I have forty-two dollars for Trevor Reynolds," Ashley said, looking at Kristi.

Kristi dug a little bit more in her bag, then sighed and rolled her eyes.

"Going once, going twice . . . sold for forty-two dollars!" Ashley called out, grinning.

Trevor turned around and hugged Mary-Kate as everyone applauded the big sale.

"Thank you! You saved me again!" he whispered into her ear, sending chills down her spine.

"Yeah. You owe me forty-two dollars," Mary-Kate told him, trying to get control of her beating heart.

"No problem. It's totally worth it," Trevor said. "Besides, this is going to be the easiest P.A. gig ever!"

"What makes you say that?" Mary-Kate asked.

Trevor blinked. "Well, it's you," he said. "You're not going to really make me *do* anything . . . right?"

Mary-Kate smiled wickedly. "Think again, personal-assistant-boy."

"Okay, was that even a test?" Ashley said as she and Felicity walked out of Mr. Smith's English class that afternoon. "I mean, name five Shakespeare plays and discuss their themes? You'd have to be brain-dead not to pass."

"I only got four. Do you think I'll at least get a B?" Felicity said.

"Felicity! You're kidding!" Ashley exclaimed. "We studied Shakespeare all year."

"Hey! My mind was on other things!" Felicity replied. "Like the fact that we need to talk about the prank."

Ashley sighed and lowered her voice to a whisper. "I still don't understand how we're going to move that big thing."

"Oh please! *We're* not going to move it," Felicity said. "We're gonna get someone else to do the heavy lifting."

"Like who?" Ashley asked.

"What about David? He's your personal assistant tomorrow, right?"

"No way. David and I are going out on a date, and spending the night with a rusty old cow is not exactly romantic," Ashley said.

"Hey, um . . . Ashley? Felicity? Would you guys sign my yearbook?"

Ashley turned to find Trina Banarjee, Sharon Allessi, and a few other sophomore girls and guys looking up at them with wide eyes. The group of younger kids were in Drama Club with Ashley and Felicity and had basically followed them around all year. They each had a yearbook clutched in their hands.

"Sure," Ashley said, digging a pen out of her bag.

"Thank you *so* much!" Sharon said, handing over her book.

"You can sign mine, too. If you want," Tony Rico said, playing it cool.

Felicity and Ashley signed their books, then watched them scurry away, excitedly comparing the entries.

Ashley grinned after them. "Felicity, I think we just found our heavy lifters," she said, starting down the hall again.

"Omigosh, you're right! The sophomores will do anything for us!" Felicity said. "You're brilliant!"

"I'm aware," Ashley joked.

"So we'll talk plans later?" Felicity asked when they reached the end of the hall.

"Absolutely. Later!" Ashley replied, turning toward her locker. *As soon as I'm done planning my date with David, working on my speech, and studying for French— just in case,* she thought.

This week was turning out to be a lot busier than she'd planned.

Felicity_girl invites Claude18, AshleyO and Mary★★★Kate to Instant Message!

Felicity_girl: Let's talk prank!

Claude18: Wait! First i wanna hear about ur date! What r u gonna do?

AshleyO: I don't know. I asked him, so do I plan the whole date?

Claude18: u didn't ASK—you bought him.

Felicity_girl: ka-CHING!!!

AshleyO: I'm serious u guys!

Mary★★★Kate: Hello? I thought u were writing ur speech!!

AshleyO: ??Where are u??

Mary★★★Kate: Dad's computer. Slacker.

AshleyO: Hey. I'm planning a DATE here!

Mary★★★Kate: OK fine. What's the dilemma?

Felicity_girl: Ash wants to know if she needs 2 open doors and order for him.

AshleyO: Ignore her. Where should we go? Should I pay?

Claude18: go dutch. be a woman of the 21st century.

AshleyO: I'm down with that.

Claude18: oops. dad wants me 2 study 4 spanish final. hasta manana!

AshleyO: Later, girls!

Felicity_girl: wait! prank??

CHAPTER THREE

Thank you, Trevor!" Mary-Kate said as he returned from the lunch line the next day, bringing her a bottle of water. She had been torturing Trevor all day, making him drive her to school, open doors for her, even carry her books. This was the third trip he had made for her since lunch started, but he was being a good sport about it.

Across the lunchroom Kristi glared at them with narrowed eyes. Feeling triumphant, Mary-Kate smiled and waved at her until she looked away.

"Anything else I can get you, boss?" Trevor asked as he sat down.

"No, that'll be all for now," Mary-Kate said.

"Good! He's gotten up so many times, I'm starting to get dizzy," Claudia said.

"Yeah, dude," Cooper put in. "You *can* say no to her."

"Hey, Mary-Kate bought me fair and square. I gotta do what the girl says," Trevor replied.

"Would you open this for me?" Mary-Kate asked innocently, handing over the water bottle. Crushing on him or not, she loved teasing Trevor. It was just so much fun.

Trevor sighed and dropped his fork, then popped the top on the bottle.

"Don't worry, Trevor," Ashley put in sympathetically. "At least there's only a couple of hours left."

"Hallelujah!" Trevor said. "Three o'clock and I'm home free!"

"I don't *think* so," Mary-Kate said. "You're my personal assistant for the *day,* not just the school day."

"Wow, man. She's tough," Cooper said.

"A girl's gotta do what a girl's gotta do," she said with a happy shrug. "And tonight I want to go to that new pizza place downtown *and* see the new Sandra Bullock movie."

"That chick flick?" Cooper said, covering his smile with one hand. "Dude, you should've let Kristi Carlton buy you!"

"No way. This is definitely the lesser evil," Trevor said. He turned to Mary-Kate and smiled. "Your wish is my command."

Butterflies raced through Mary-Kate's stomach. This was her big chance. A real date with Trevor. Of course, he didn't know it was a date, but that didn't make it any less exciting. They were going to be alone together for dinner and a movie. That was all that mattered.

"Great," she said with a grin. "Pick me up at seven."

•   •   •

Mary-Kate stared at herself in the bathroom mirror that evening, trying desperately to fluff her hair. Unfortunately it seemed determined to hang flat. Why did her mousse work some times and totally tank on her at others?

"Mary-Kate! Trevor's going to be here in fifteen minutes, and you still haven't gotten dressed!" Ashley called from Mary-Kate's bedroom. "I think an hour on your hair is more than enough."

Mary-Kate sighed and walked down the hall to her room. Ashley had already laid out three outfits for her on the bed. Sometimes she really didn't know how she would get ready for dates without her sister.

"It's all stringy," Mary-Kate said, slipping out of her robe.

"It looks perfect," her sister told her. "And besides, why are you stressing? It's just Trevor."

Yeah, just the love of my life, Mary-Kate thought. She looked at Ashley and for a split second thought about telling her how much this night actually meant, but she stopped herself. Usually she told Ashley everything, but this was different. She wanted to find out how Trevor felt before she put herself out there and let everyone else know about her feelings.

"I'm just having a bad-hair day," she said, snagging the tank top her sister held toward her. "And you know how I feel about bad-hair days."

"Totally," Ashley said sympathetically. "Bad-hair days should definitely be considered sick days."

"Hey, I like this!" Mary-Kate said, buttoning up her long denim skirt and checking her reflection. "Good work! What're you going to wear for your date with David?"

"I was thinking I'd pick one of the outfits you turned down," Ashley said with a smile. "Thank you for not taking the little black dress!"

"Eh, you look better in it than I do anyway," Mary-Kate said, picking it up and tossing it at Ashley.

She was trying to act casual. She had to see how the date went first, but she was hoping she'd get up the courage to tell Trevor how she really felt. She'd only been wanting to do it for years.

It's going to be great, she told herself, turning in front of the mirror for a side view. *You'll be just fine.*

The doorbell rang, and Mary-Kate's heart jumped into her throat.

"That's him! Have fun!" Ashley said, zipping up the dress.

Mary-Kate grabbed her sister in a hug, needing the support.

"What was that for?" Ashley asked with a laugh.

"For good luck! With David!" Mary-Kate told her.

"Thanks!" Ashley called after her as Mary-Kate hurried downstairs.

"Here goes nothing," Mary-Kate whispered. Then

she wiped her palms on her skirt and opened the door.

Trevor looked perfect. He was wearing fine-waled cords, a clean T-shirt with no graphic on it, and a pair of actual shoes. Not sneakers, not sandals, but shoes. It even appeared that he had combed his normally stylishly-mussed hair. This was dressed up by Trevor standards.

"Wow," Trevor said, his eyes opening wide. "You look—"

Mary-Kate flushed and Trevor swallowed hard.

"What did you do to yourself?" he asked.

"Me? Nothing!" Mary-Kate said with a shrug. Trevor had complimented her! Well, practically. And he was all dressed up. Was it possible that he considered this a real date as well?

She followed him to the Jeep. He opened the door for her, and she stepped in, unable to control her grin. This was definitely going to be a night to remember.

"I gotta tell you, Ashley, when you bid on me at the auction yesterday, I never thought we'd be going out on a date!" David said, reaching across the table and putting a hand on top of one of hers.

Ashley forced a smile as she tried to think of a way to remove her hand without offending him. This should have been the perfect date. They were sitting at a window table at The Bluffs, a romantic restaurant overlooking the ocean. But somehow there were just no sparks. David Ryan was a dud.

Thinking fast, Ashley faked a sneeze, using both hands to cover her face.

"Bless you!" David said.

"Thanks."

Ashley lowered her hands into her lap. She looked at David over the flickering candle on their table, trying to summon up some of the attraction she'd felt toward him just yesterday. With dark hair, dark eyes, and a tall, lanky frame, he was definitely still cute—that hadn't changed. But though he was fun to be around in school, in a one-on-one situation he was just a little too much. Too loud, too overbearing, cracking jokes every other second. It was like sitting at a sophisticated restaurant with a stand-up comic.

A champagne cork popped behind David and he hit the floor. "Take cover!" he joked, holding his napkin up to indicate surrender. Then he cracked up laughing. The couple next to them looked at him as if he were insane.

Oh, God, help me! Ashley thought, mortified.

This was going to be a very long night.

"Your munchies, madame," Trevor said, returning to his seat in the movie theater just as the previews started.

Mary-Kate's eyes widened at the sheer volume of food he'd brought back. All her favorites—popcorn with loads of butter, plain M&Ms, and Swedish Fish, along with a Coke the size of California. He handed her the box of Swedish Fish, and she sighed happily.

Trevor knew her so well! Clearly they were meant to be together.

"So what's this movie about again?" Trevor asked, settling in.

"Standard romantic-comedy formula," Mary-Kate said. "Girl wants boy, boy wants girl, some big obstacle gets in their way and they conquer it."

She smiled at his profile. He looked so cute tonight. And in the dim light from the screen, the hushed atmosphere of the theater, she almost felt as if she could lean toward him and kiss him. What would he do? How would he react? Would he kiss back?

Okay, forget kissing. Just say *something. Tell him how you feel,* Mary-Kate told herself. Her skin tingled all over, and her heart was in her throat.

"Trevor? There's something I've been wanting to ask you. No, *tell* you . . ."

Trevor tossed a couple of kernels of popcorn into his mouth and started to cough.

"Are you okay? Are you choking?" Mary-Kate asked.

Trevor shook his head no and took a long slug of his soda. "Sorry. Just went down the wrong pipe," he said with a few more coughs.

Oookay. You finally try to tell him, and he almost chokes, Mary-Kate thought, returning her attention to the screen. *That can't be a good sign.*

"What did you want to tell me?" he asked.

"Oh, um, just . . . thanks for the snacks," she said,

feeling lame, but the moment had already passed.

As the movie began, Trevor put his elbow on the armrest he and Mary-Kate were sharing, and their skin touched. An insanely intense shot of energy sizzled up Mary-Kate's side. Her instinct was to move her arm away, but Trevor didn't, so she didn't either. She couldn't believe how much it affected her just to have their forearms touching.

I bet he has really soft lips, Mary-Kate thought, her mind in a hazy fog. *I bet if I kissed him, he'd taste just like that cinnamon gum he's always popping. I bet he'd put his arms around me and hold me close and . . .*

Someone kicked the back of Mary-Kate's seat and she jumped, letting out a yelp.

"Oops! Sorry," the guy behind her said.

"Oh . . . no problem," Mary-Kate replied, turning crimson from the thought of her daydream.

"Everything okay?" Trevor asked.

Mary-Kate could barely rip her gaze off his lips.

"Uh . . . yeah. Everything's fine," she replied, forcing herself to turn toward the screen. Suddenly she knew there was no way she would be able to concentrate on the movie.

"So . . ." David said, looking at Ashley from the passenger seat of the SUV she shared with Mary-Kate. They were parked in front of his house after dinner, which Ashley was still amazed she had survived.

"So . . ." she replied, every muscle in her body taut.

Don't try to kiss me! Please don't try to kiss me! she thought.

"I had a great time," David said with a smile. "I'm very glad you bought me."

Ashley faked a laugh. She was so tense, it came out sounding like a snort. David was a nice guy, but she just wasn't attracted to him. She knew that if he kissed her, she would freeze up, and it would be totally awkward. Even more awkward than *this* moment was.

"Well, thanks, Ashley," David said, unbuckling his seat belt and getting out of the car. "We should do it again sometime."

The door slammed and Ashley had never felt so relieved in her life. He hadn't made a move on her! It was as if all the air in the car was suddenly hers again. She looked at David through the window and realized he was watching her expectantly.

Omigosh! What do I say? "No, we shouldn't do it again?" I can't say that.

Part of her wanted to just pull away from the curb, but she couldn't do it. He was standing right there!

"Yes, definitely!" Ashley blurted out in a panic, unable to stop her tongue. "I'll call you!"

She saw David's smile brighten as she slammed the car into gear and pulled out. She couldn't believe what had just happened.

"I'll call you!"? Ugh! What was I thinking?!

AshleyO invites Felicity_girl, trina16, Bobbo-robb, *19rico and SharonAllessi to Instant Message!

AshleyO: All right, peeps. U R the
    chosen ones. We want u 2 help out
    with this year's senior prank.
Bobbo-robb: COOL! Whatever, wherever!
trina16: U don't even know what she
    wants us 2 do! It could be illegal!
Felicity_girl: sophomores, sophomores.
    we would never ask u to do anything
    illegal.
*19rico: does it involve a panty raid?
AshleyO: Why would it involve—
SharonAllessi: Ignore him. He was the
    king of panty raids at camp.
*19rico: watch it, Sharon! i still have
    ur underroos from 3rd grade.
Felicity_girl: can we focus here,
    people??? school parking lot,
    wednesday at midnight.
AshleyO: Got it?
Bobbo-robb: we're there.
trina16: i don't know. . . .
Bobbo-robb: don't worry, she'll show!
AshleyO: It'll be fun, Trina! The Class
    of 2004 thanks u! Signing off!

CHAPTER FOUR

Trevor pulled his Jeep to a stop in front of the Olsen's house and put it into park. Mary-Kate felt suddenly self-conscious, as she did at the end of every date. It was like a reflex reaction—wondering what to say and whether there would be a kiss.

Only this time it was ten times more torturous. Because this time it was Trevor, the guy she liked more than she'd ever liked any guy before. Unfortunately it didn't matter how much she liked him. No way was he was going to kiss her.

"I can't believe we just did dinner and a movie," Trevor said, glancing at her. "Isn't that, like, standard first-date stuff?"

Mary-Kate wanted to leap with joy. He'd said *date*! He was handing her the perfect opportunity to tell him how she felt—that she had been pretending it was a real date all along. "Yeah. I know," she said, toying nervously with her purse strap. "I bet people thought we were a couple."

Let's see how he reacts to that idea, she thought.

"Totally," he said, running his finger along the steering wheel. "Imagine if this were a real date. I'd probably kiss you good night right about now."

Mary-Kate's heart slammed against her rib cage. She looked at him, her face flushed. She felt as if her insides were puddling together. *Does he like me? Does he really like me, too?* she wondered.

"If this were a real date, I'd probably kiss you back," she said, barely able to get the words out.

She locked eyes with Trevor, wishing she could tell what he was thinking. His gaze was so intense, she felt for a split second that he was actually going to do it. That he was going to lean forward and kiss her.

Omigosh! This is it! Mary-Kate thought excitedly.

Then Trevor laughed. He turned and looked out through the windshield. "Us. Kissing. That's funny."

Something inside Mary-Kate collapsed. The whole thing was a joke to him! How had she misread him?

"Yeah. Funny," she said. Somehow she managed to smile, pretending that she had been kidding as well. "Well, see you tomorrow."

"Yeah, see ya!" Trevor replied.

Mary-Kate got out of the Jeep and shut the door, disappointment welling up inside her. She could have sworn he was feeling the same way she was in that moment, but clearly she was wrong. Trevor waved and pulled into the road, blasting his stereo and leaving Mary-Kate to wonder if she'd really imagined it all.

• • •

Ashley washed her face, changed into her pj's, and sat down in front of her vanity mirror. She was dotting moisturizer on her forehead when, in the mirror, she saw Mary-Kate walk in and flop onto her bed.

"What's up? How did it go?" Ashley asked, turning in her seat. She had seen her sister upset before, but this was different. This seemed serious.

"If I tell you, you swear you won't laugh?" Mary-Kate said, staring straight up at the ceiling.

"Of course," Ashley said.

Mary-Kate sat up, took a deep breath, and looked at Ashley tentatively. "I thought Trevor was going to kiss me just now . . . and he didn't."

"Omigosh! I knew it!" Ashley said, jumping up. "I *knew* you were too freaked about this whole pseudo-date thing! You *like* Trevor!"

"You promised you wouldn't laugh!" Mary-Kate said.

"I'm not laughing!" Ashley said. "I'm just saying it's about time! Have I not always told you that you and Trevor would be perfect together?"

Mary-Kate sighed, her shoulders slumping. "Yeah, you have," she said. "But I don't think it's gonna happen anyway."

"Why? Did you tell him how you feel?" Ashley asked, sitting down on the bed next to her sister.

"No. I chickened out," Mary-Kate said.

"Well, you have to tell him," Ashley said. "Give the guy a chance. You *know* he loves you."

"Yeah, but as a friend," Mary-Kate said, the vulnerability in her eyes obvious. "What if I tell him, and he doesn't feel the same way? It could ruin everything. Things would never be the same between us."

Ashley frowned, thinking that over. Her sister had a point. Guys could be pretty nuts when they felt trapped or pressured. She wrapped an arm around Mary-Kate, and Mary-Kate put her head on her shoulder.

"Don't worry," Ashley said. "We'll think of something." They sat for a moment in silence, and then her sister's head popped up.

"Hey! How was *your* date?" Mary-Kate asked, pulling one leg up on the bed so she could face Ashley.

"Only okay," Ashley said with a shrug. "Definitely not a love connection."

"Lame night for both of us, huh?" Mary-Kate said with a sympathetic smile.

"You could say that," Ashley replied. "But I still have three more guys to ask out, so who knows? Anything can happen! Anything can happen for *both* of us."

AshleyO invites Felicity_girl to Instant Message!

Felicity_girl: soooo? how wuz it?

AshleyO: Awful. Well, not awful. Just
. . . eh. David's okay, I definitey
don't see it going anywhere.

Felicity_girl: ouch! sorry girl! but
these things happen.

AshleyO: Yeah, but I said I'd call him.

Felicity_girl: u did? Y?

AshleyO: I don't KNOW! WHY did I say
I'd call him???

Felicity_girl: CHILL! u were probably
just being ur supernice self. knew
that would get u in trouble 1 day.

AshleyO: LOL. OK. But what do I do now?

Felicity_girl: just don't call him.
guys do it all the time!!! they NEED
a dose of their own medicine!

AshleyO: I don't know. . . .

Felicity_girl: trust me, chica. he'll
get the message. david may be
immature, but he's not stupid. i
know. i copied off his trig test
last month. got my first A in that
class.

AshleyO: WHAT!?!?!?!

Felicity_girl: kidding!!!

CHAPTER FIVE

Ashley sat on the gym floor with Claudia after school the next day, working on decorations for the prom. She had been active on the prom committee for months now, and she couldn't believe it was less than two weeks away. The school year was really coming to a close. *High school* was coming to a close. It was all very exciting but bittersweet at the same time.

"Hey, Ashley. What are you thinking about?"

Ashley blinked and looked up to find Hunter Robeson hovering over her. Hunter was a totally artistic type with light brown skin, crazy-curly brown hair with blond highlights, and the most stunning green eyes. She was surprised to find them focused on her.

"Oh . . . you know. School ending and all that," Ashley said with a casual shrug. "I guess I spaced out."

"Well, you guys are doing a good job on the plane," Hunter said, looking over their work.

"Thanks," Claudia said. "I think it'll work."

Ashley smiled as she finished painting the cardboard propeller in front of her. Hunter had come up with their prom theme—*Casablanca*—back at their first meeting. The centerpiece was a huge airplane constructed out of plywood, papier mâché, and cardboard.

"*Casablanca* is the most romantic movie ever," he had said. "I can't think of a better theme for the most romantic night of high school."

Ashley had started crushing on him way back then. She thought it would be amazing to go out with him, but time had flown by, and now here they were—a week and a half away from the end of school.

"I'm going to go get some snacks from the vending machine. You guys want anything?" Hunter asked.

"I'll go with you," Ashley said, getting to her feet.

Claudia grinned and mouthed, *"Good luck!"*

"So, are you a chocolate-type girl or a chip-type girl?" Hunter asked, loading coins into the machine.

"Actually I'm more of a pretzel type," Ashley said.

"I like pretzel girls," Hunter said with a smile.

Ashley grinned. She took a deep breath and decided to go for it. No mixed signals like with Todd, no games like with David. She was just going to ask.

"Listen, Hunter, I was wondering if you might want to go out with me . . . sometime," she said. She tilted her head and smiled, trying to keep the butterflies in her stomach from bursting free.

Hunter's whole face lit up. "Yeah? I mean . . . yeah. That would be cool."

"Cool!" Ashley said. But then she immediately

froze up. Should she press him for a day and time or would that look too desperate?

"Actually I have tickets to this play tomorrow night," Hunter told her. "My sister was supposed to go with me, but she has to work. Are you interested?"

"Sure!" Ashley said happily. "I love good theater."

"Great," Hunter said, his smile widening. "Then I'll pick you up around seven?"

"Perfect," Ashley said.

He pulled out a bag of pretzels from the vending machine and handed it to her, his eyes sparkling.

Ashley flushed and looked at the ground. She was definitely getting better at this asking-guys-out thing.

"Okay, we've got every yearbook from the past fifty years," Trevor said, sitting on the floor of the library next to Mary-Kate. The volumes were stacked up all around them. "What are we looking for again?"

"Anything," Mary-Kate whispered, pulling a book from the pile at random. "I was thinking that if I'm going to start a new tradition, it would be cool if it had some kind of historical significance, you know? Something we could tie back to other classes."

Trevor opened a binder full of old copies of the *Vista*, the school newspaper. "Wow. You're really taking this new-tradition thing seriously," he said.

"Well, it's my one crazy thing," Mary-Kate said, burying her nose in the yearbook. Ashley was the only one who knew that asking Trevor out was her *real* resolution, so she wasn't about to blow her cover by not going forward with the new-tradition thing.

At least Trevor had offered to help. Working on this would give them even more time together. More opportunities for Mary-Kate to tell him how she felt.

"I had a really good time last night, by the way," Trevor said as he leafed through the old newspapers.

Mary-Kate's heart thumped. That was the type of thing a person said after a *date*, not after a night of hanging out with a best friend. She looked up at him, almost afraid to see if she was right. Trevor gazed back at her, and it was as if time had stopped. He slowly smiled, and it wasn't his goofy grin or teasing smirk. It was a small, personal smile. It was different than any smile Trevor had ever given her.

Before Mary-Kate knew what was happening, Trevor reached out and gently brushed her hair away from her eyes.

This was it. This was *definitely* it.

At that very moment Kristi Carlton came around the corner into their aisle. Trevor yanked his hand away and tucked his bare feet under his legs Indian-style. Kristi paused, and Mary-Kate felt hollow and numb. What had almost happened?

I'm never going to know, she realized.

"What're you guys doing here?" Kristi asked.

Almost kissing, Mary-Kate thought sarcastically. *But not, thanks to you.*

"It's secret class business," Trevor replied. "We could tell you, but then we'd have to kill you."

Mary-Kate laughed, surprising herself considering how awful she felt, and Kristi shot them a dirty look before walking away. The whole encounter lasted two seconds, but the damage had been done. Trevor was looking in his binder again, and the potential-kiss moment was definitely over.

Frustrated, Mary-Kate flipped through the yearbook for 1986, barely seeing anything before her. She got to the middle, where the senior class picture was. There was the entire class in their caps and gowns, sitting in the bleachers by the football field. It looked just like every other graduation picture she'd seen except that the girls' hair was bigger and a lot of the boys had mullets. She was about to close the book when she noticed the banner hanging across the bleachers.

The banner read OCEAN VIEW HIGH in the center, and around the words were dozens of dates sewn at different angles and in different patterns. It looked as if every class from 1959 on up was represented—all the way up to that year's class, 1985. Since the group photos were taken on graduation day, they only made it into the following year's yearbook.

"Hey. Check this out," Mary-Kate said, sliding toward Trevor. He bent over the book, his face so close to hers she could smell his cinnamon gum.

Focus, Mary-Kate thought. *We may have something.*

"That's so cool," Trevor said. "It looks like every class got to add their own year with their own motif."

"Have you ever seen it before?" Mary-Kate asked.

"Never," Trevor admitted. "What do you think happened to it?"

"I don't know," Mary-Kate said. She grabbed a couple of yearbooks and handed them to him. "You check years before '86, and I'll check years after."

With an air of excitement Mary-Kate and Trevor hit the books. Mary-Kate flipped to the center of the 1987 book, and, sure enough, there it was. The same banner was strung in front of the class, but now a *1986* had been added near the center.

"It's in all of these," Trevor said, opening book after book. "It goes all the way back through the sixties."

Mary-Kate excitedly opened the next few books and found the banner in the photos for 1987, 1988, and 1989. But when she opened the 1991 book with the graduating class of 1990 in it, the banner was gone. She grabbed 1992, 1993, and so on, but the banner never reappeared.

"They stopped using it after 1989," Mary-Kate said.

"Why? It's so cool-looking," Trevor said, bringing a 1960's book close to his face to study the grainy photo. "I'd love to have this for our senior picture."

Mary-Kate grinned. "Then we have a mission," she said. "Let's find out what happened to the banner."

Trevor86 invites Mary***Kate to Instant Message!

Trevor86: U are going 2 love this.
    There's a ballot in the April 1990
    Vista asking seniors 2 vote on
    whether they want the school banner
    used in their class picture.
Mary***Kate: They VOTED on it?
Trevor86: It was a big deal, because in
    the next issue there's a story about
    how the banner was voted out and 2
    opinion pieces over why it's good
    that it's gone and why it's bad.
Mary***Kate: Seriously??? Why good?
Trevor86: The girl who wrote against it
    says it's a new decade, time 2 move
    on. She says it smells funny. :)
Mary***Kate: !!! Do u think they threw
    it away?
Trevor86: I don't know. We'll have 2 do
    more research. This is kind of fun.
Mary***Kate: I know! I feel like a P.I.
    Let's keep this a secret. I want it
    2 be a surprise if we find it.
Trevor86: Lips zipped. Promise.
Mary***Kate: Cool. Thanks for helping!
Trevor86: Anything for u, MK!

CHAPTER SIX

This is so cool," Ashley whispered as she, Felicity, and Claudia slipped out of Felicity's father's pickup on Wednesday night. It was late, and she could barely see the silhouette of the old, broken-down farmhouse in the distance.

"I can't believe we're doing this," Claudia said, pulling a baseball cap over her freshly-dyed red hair.

"Believe it, baby!" Ashley said. "*Carpe diem!*"

"What happened to Mary-Kate?" Felicity asked.

"She's researching her new tradition," Ashley said, tucking her own wavy locks under a dark knit cap she'd snagged from her dad's ski wardrobe. "Too bad. She would've loved this."

Ashley and her friends were each dressed in head-to-toe black, perfect for midnight cow-stealing. They waited by the truck until about ten sophomores joined them, having come from their parking spots farther down the road.

"Why did we have to park a mile away again?" some tall kid with braces asked.

"Looks less suspicious," Felicity told them.

"I don't get it. If Crusty doesn't belong to anybody, why are we being all stealthy about it?" Claudia asked Ashley as they followed the rest of the crowd toward the rusty old cow.

"This way at least we have a chance of going unseen and avoiding any explanation at all," Ashley said. "And besides, the whole black spy-gear thing is very now," she added, sucking in her cheeks, model-style.

Claudia laughed as they gathered around the cow. The rusty hunk of metal was about a foot taller than the tallest person there and at least six feet long. Up close it was a lot bigger than Ashley had thought. She was already nervous, what with the midnight prank vibe in the air. But now that she realized how impossible the task looked, her heart started to pound all over again.

"Okay, everyone grab hold wherever you can," Felicity instructed. "Let's see how heavy this puppy is."

Ashley grabbed a leg with Claudia, and counted to three. Everyone strained as hard as they could—and managed to lift the cow an inch off the ground.

"Okay, new plan!" Ashley announced as they dropped the metal hulk. "Tip and drag!"

Together they pushed the cow over onto its side, and a few of the sophomores dragged it toward the truck. Ashley and her friends walked behind, letting the younger kids do the work. Suddenly they saw a flash of light and everyone froze.

"Car!" Claudia announced, sending the group running for cover. A couple of kids hid behind the truck, while others just hit the ground. Ashley, Claudia, and Felicity crouched in the bushes. They held their breath as the car zoomed by.

"Coast's clear," Ashley said.

Wow, I really am kicking the Goody-Two-Shoes rep, Ashley thought with pride. Instead of being the responsible valedictorian, here she was, out in the middle of the night, committing rusty-cow-theft.

"Come on," she said to the group by the truck. "Let's do some liftin'. Head 'em up and move 'em out!"

They all got to work, inching the cow over to the truck. They pulled down the ramp used for heavy loading and maneuvered the cow onto it. They started to push her up, but it was slow going. A couple of guys crawled into the truck bed to pull while everyone else pushed. About halfway up the cow started to slide to one side a bit, and the two guys who were pulling from the truck bed lost control.

"Watch out!" Ashley shouted.

But it was too late. Crusty slipped right off the side of the ramp and hit the ground with a sickening crack. Everyone jumped back. Ashley squeezed her eyes shut, and when she opened them again, Crusty's head lay about three feet from her body, staring up at them with blank eyes. It was a sorry sight indeed.

"Oh no!" Ashley said.

"We beheaded Crusty!" Felicity shouted.

Ashley looked at her friends, and everyone cracked up laughing.

"Oh . . . my . . . gosh!" Mary-Kate said as she drove the SUV up the school driveway on Thursday morning. "You guys totally outdid yourselves!"

At least half the student population was gathered in the courtyard at the center of the school, milling around the picnic tables and benches that peppered the area. All of them were looking up at Crusty, who stood on top of the old, filled-in fountain right in the middle of the yard.

In the daylight she looked about ten times better than she had the night before. Ashley and Felicity had reattached her head, using an entire roll of duct tape. They had painted a football jersey on her in green and yellow with the name *Crusty* across the back and the number *04* for the class year. She wore a bunch of leis around her neck to hide the duct tape and a pair of huge pink sunglasses on her snout.

Mary-Kate parked the car, and together they walked to the courtyard. A few people came up to Ashley and whispered their congratulations. Ashley was surprised they had already heard who was responsible, but she was sure she had the sophomores to thank for that.

"Nice job, Ashley! I didn't know you had it in you!" Meredith said under her breath.

"The valedictorian is a master prankster!" Danny Ring added.

Kristi Carlton walked by with her friends and shot Ashley a grudging smile. "Not bad," she said.

"Thanks," Ashley replied. Coming from Kristi that was major praise.

"Well?" Felicity said, sauntering over. "What do you think of your new rebel status?"

"I like it," Ashley said with a grin.

"You know, you're really sticking to your resolution," Mary-Kate said, impressed. "Asking out guys, planning dates, stealing cows . . ."

"Hey! *Carpe diem!*" Ashley said happily.

"Okay," Felicity said, putting a hand on Ashley's shoulder. "You *need* to stop saying that."

"According to my research, back in the fifties they used to order a new graduation banner every year," Mary-Kate explained to Trevor that afternoon. "But in 1960 the budget wasn't big enough, so the class took the banner from the year before and sewed their own year onto it. After that it became a tradition, lasting all the way up to '89."

"Then in 1990 they voted it down, and the banner disappeared," Trevor said, pausing in front of the art wing closet.

"So . . . what? You really think it's in here?" Mary-Kate asked, eyeing the door.

Trevor whipped a huge ring of keys from his pocket. "Well, Mr. Viola let me in here once to get some supplies, and there's all kinds of crazy stuff back there. He agreed that if it's anywhere, it's in this closet."

He flicked on the lights, and Mary-Kate's jaw dropped. The closet was huge and packed with stuff. Shelves overflowed with boxes of paper, felt, clay, huge bottles of glue, paints, brushes, and everything else imaginable.

"Back here," Trevor said.

Mary-Kate followed him into the back of the closet. The last shelf was stacked with random relics of school spirit. A huge seagull head from a mascot's costume teetered at one end. Crumpled pom-poms were shoved into dusty megaphones.

"Check it out," Mary-Kate said, pulling down an old varsity jacket. "Varsity baseball, 1974."

"Someone's been cold for about thirty years," Trevor joked. He crouched down and pulled a box off the bottom shelf. It hit the floor with a thud. "Here. Check this one."

Mary-Kate kneeled on the floor and opened the box. It was filled with folded-up cloth, and her pulse raced with excitement. She pulled out a banner, but when she unfolded it, it read *Welcome Back, Principal Lawrence!*

"Who's Principal Lawrence?" she asked, putting the banner aside.

"He's that one in the yearbooks from the sixties.

You know, with the wacky sideburns?" Trevor said, yanking out another box. "What's in here?"

Mary-Kate caught a glimpse of some gingham fabric, then a hint of silver.

"Omigosh! I think this is it!" she cried, standing up.

Trevor grinned and got to his feet as well. Together they unfurled the banner, laying it out on the floor. The various years were sewn on everywhere and every which way. The *1969* had a peace sign sewn behind it. The *1980* had Olympic rings around it. The *1972* was all multicolored and swirly. The banner was dusty and wrinkled, but it was beautiful.

"Jackpot," Trevor said with a grin.

Mary-Kate smiled back at him.

"You know what? I'm glad we're doing this together," Trevor said.

Mary-Kate's skin tingled with goose bumps at his heartfelt words. "Yeah," she said. "Me, too."

"Hunter, that play was amazing!" Ashley said. "Thank you so much for bringing me."

"I'm glad you liked it," Hunter replied as he paid for their coffees at the café next to the theater. "Not everyone would understand a piece like that."

Ashley beamed as she moved toward the bustling coffee shop. She didn't know why anyone wouldn't understand the play they had just seen. It was so romantic—so heartbreaking and so uplifting at the same time. She had already decided that she really had to start seeing more theater.

Hunter sat down across the table from Ashley and slid her coffee to her. Then he offered her the cream and sugar before taking any for himself. Not only was this guy cute and creative, he was polite as well.

"You know, the man who wrote that play was exiled from his country because the government thought it was too racy," Hunter said.

"*That* play?" Ashley asked. "The characters barely even kissed."

"I know. We're lucky we live in a country that allows free speech," Hunter said, sipping his coffee. "The playwright, Kristov Ladimir, lives here now and writes whatever he wants without worrying whether he'll be hauled off to jail."

"Wow," Ashley said.

Hunter kept impressing her. Now she realized he was cute, creative, polite, *and* smart. Plus the guy definitely knew how to dress for a date. He was wearing a pair of pressed pants and an olive-green button-down shirt that brought out the color of his eyes. It was totally different than the hippie-artist gear he usually wore, but he hadn't completely ditched his style. His curls still stuck out adorably at every angle, and his shoes were spattered with paint from prom committee.

"Hey! Hunter, my man!"

"Hey, Josh!" Hunter got up to slap hands with a tall

African-American guy approaching their table. Another guy with long hair and a girl with spiky blond locks followed. "Hey, everyone! This is Ashley," Hunter said. "Ashley, this is Josh, Mitchell, and Marisol."

"Hi," Ashley said. "Do you guys want to join us?"

"We wouldn't want to intrude," Marisol said.

"No! It's okay," Hunter said as he and Ashley slid over. "Were you all at the play?"

"Yeah! Wasn't it *so* amazing?" Marisol asked, plopping down next to Ashley.

"Ladimir is intense," Mitchell added. "I've seen this piece three times already."

"Really?" Ashley asked.

"Yep," Josh put in. "Was this your first time?"

"Yeah," Ashley replied. "I guess I'm the new girl."

"That's good!" Marisol said brightly. "It's great that you're willing to expose yourself to new things."

"Thanks," Ashley said, smiling.

That kind of sounded like her *carpe diem* philosophy. She took a sip of her coffee as the conversation continued around her. Hunter was great, his friends were cool, and she knew that whatever she did with him would be an experience. She found herself already looking forward to their next date.

Tonight when I say "I'll call you," I'm definitely going to mean it, she thought.

AshleyO invites Felicity_girl to Instant Message!

AshleyO: No more finals!!!
    Whooo-hooo!!!
Felicity_girl: and tomorrow is senior
    cut day, baby!!!
AshleyO: Yes! So we'll pick u up at 8 2
    go 2 Adventure Mountain.
Felicity_girl: 8!!??? i don't get up at
    8 on a school day!!!
AshleyO: F, school starts at 8:15.
Felicity_girl: exactly!
AshleyO: It's an hour drive. We want to
    get there before the lines get huge.
Felicity_girl: do we have to do this?
    seniors do this every year. y don't
    we do something different?
AshleyO: OK. Like what?
AshleyO: I'm waiting . . .
Felicity_girl: ummm . . . sleep late?
AshleyO: I'll see u at 8.

CHAPTER SEVEN

So, Ashley, have you decided who you're going to the prom with yet?" Claudia asked Friday morning on their drive to Adventure Mountain.

Mary-Kate tilted her head to look at her sister from the passenger seat. She was also curious.

"I'm keeping my options open," Ashley said, her eyes on the road. "But Hunter is a definite possibility."

"Well, we all know who I'm going with. Having a boyfriend doesn't leave many options," Claudia joked. "What about you, Felicity?"

Mary-Kate turned around to look at Felicity, who was slouched in her seat. A pair of dark glasses covered her eyes, and she had the hood of her sweatshirt pulled up to shield herself from the sun.

"It's too early in the morning to talk prom dates," she said with a yawn.

Mary-Kate laughed. "Whoever he is, he'll have to be able to handle your falling asleep on the dance floor."

"Hey! I'm a night person! When it comes to the prom, I will be ready to go!" Felicity said. "I just wish

I could go with someone I *really* liked. You know, like Claudia is doing."

"And Mary-Kate," Ashley said.

Mary-Kate's heart hit the floor of the car, and she glared at Ashley, wide-eyed. *She did not just say that!*

"What? I thought Mary-Kate was going with Trevor," Claudia said. She and Felicity popped their heads between the two front seats.

Suddenly Mary-Kate wished she could disappear. Ashley realized her misstep and shot Mary-Kate an apologetic look.

"I . . . I am," Mary-Kate said, her face burning.

"Hold the phone!" Felicity demanded, waving a hand between the seats. "You *like* Trevor?"

"I can't believe this! Since when?" Claudia cried.

"You guys, can we just drop this?" Mary-Kate asked, staring out the windshield. The cat was out of the bag, but that didn't mean she had to feed the thing.

"No, we can*not* drop it! This is *huge*!" Felicity exclaimed. "Does he know?"

"No, he doesn't," Mary-Kate said, embarrassed. This was all they were going to talk about for the rest of the trip. She couldn't believe Ashley had blabbed.

I may actually have to kill my sister, Mary-Kate fumed.

"Omigosh! You have to tell him! You guys would make the perfect couple!" Claudia said.

"Yes! You have to tell him today!" Felicity added. "It would be perfect! You can get him into the Tunnel of Love, and then, where it goes around the turn and gets really, really dark, you can tell him how you feel!"

"I bet he kisses you right there," Claudia said.

"You guys, you guys!" Mary-Kate said finally. "You're getting a little carried away." She turned around in her seat to look at them. "And besides, the Tunnel of Love? That's the cheesiest thing I've ever heard."

"Well, actually . . . " Ashley said, biting her lip.

"Not you, too," Mary-Kate said.

"I don't know . . . I think it's kind of cute," Ashley said with a shrug, her hands still gripping the steering wheel. "And what's wrong with today? *Carpe diem!*"

Mary-Kate and her friends groaned.

"Come on. How can Trevor even think about turning you down when you confess your feelings in the Tunnel of Love?" Claudia asked.

"Yeah! Besides, do you have any better ideas?" Felicity put in with her don't-try-to-challenge-me stare.

Mary-Kate took a deep breath and let it out noisily. "No," she said reluctantly. "Actually I don't."

Ashley and Mary-Kate waited on line for the Looping Lizard roller coaster while Claudia and Felicity took their tenth turn on the Tilt-a-Whirl. As the line inched forward, Ashley saw David on the other side of the partition and coming right toward her.

"I'm trapped," Ashley said to Mary-Kate under her breath, nodding toward David.

David's friends were looking up at the loops of the coaster, debating how long the ride was. David grinned at Ashley and waved as the line moved again.

"Hey, Ashley, Mary-Kate," he said when he got closer. "You're a hard person to get a hold of, Ashley."

"I . . . I know," Ashley said, looking around for an escape, but none was possible. She was trapped in a maze surrounded by hundreds of people. She had to make up an excuse. "My cell phone's been acting weird and I . . . I didn't get your messages until this morning."

She glanced at Mary-Kate, who looked away quickly, knowing Ashley was telling a lie.

"That's okay," David said with a shrug. "But listen, I have these tickets to the Buzzkill concert tonight. I was wondering if you wanted to come."

"Buzzkill? That's my favorite band!" Ashley exclaimed before she could doublethink it.

"Then you're in?" David asked.

Suddenly Ashley realized what she was doing. She was agreeing to a second date with a guy she didn't really like. But it was a chance to see Buzzkill. How could she pass that up?

"Yes. I'm in," she said, deciding to deal with the fallout later.

David grinned hugely, and the line started to move again. "Great! Well, then, I'll pick you up around seven?"

"Sounds like a plan!" Ashley called over her shoulder as she stepped forward.

"Ashley!" Mary-Kate hissed once David was out of hearing range.

"What?" Ashley asked innocently.

"What was that? What about Hunter?" Mary-Kate asked. "I thought you didn't want to date David again."

"It's not a date. It's a concert," Ashley said, knowing she sounded lame.

"Right," Mary-Kate said with a smirk. "Do you even believe that line?"

No, Ashley thought. But she *really* wanted to go.

"Look, a rock concert isn't exactly romantic," Ashley reasoned. "And besides, this whole thing is about living life to the fullest. And that's what I'm doing. In fact . . ."

At that moment she saw Joe Laudadia, the hottest guy in their class, winding his way toward them in the line. Joe had won Best Looking *and* Best Smile. Ashley's heart pounded as he drew closer.

"Hey, Joe!" she said.

"Hey, Ashley," he replied, flashing that grin.

"Listen, I know this is out of nowhere, but would you like to go out with me sometime?" Ashley asked.

Somehow the grin widened. "Absolutely," he said, turning to walk backward as the line moved on. "My e-mail's in the class directory!"

"Cool!" she shouted back. Then she grinned at Mary-Kate, who rolled her eyes but smiled back.

"You are definitely living life," she admitted.

• • •

"This is it," Claudia whispered into Mary-Kate's ear as they reached the head of the line at the Tunnel of Love that afternoon. "Are you ready?"

Mary-Kate looked up at Trevor's profile as he chatted with Cooper. After a few rides they had met up with the guys at lunch, and Mary-Kate was now regretting the hot dog she'd chowed down. She might be the first person ever to get sick on the totally tame Tunnel of Love ride.

"You ready?" Felicity whispered to her.

"I think so," Mary-Kate replied. *Okay, I have to do this,* she thought. She grabbed Trevor's arm before he could step into the next open car.

"You're not planning on riding in a heart-shaped car with Cooper, are you?" Mary-Kate asked.

"You have a point," Trevor said.

Claudia took Cooper's hand and snagged the car. Mary-Kate led Trevor to the one behind it. Her hands started to sweat as she took her seat.

"You're not coming?" Trevor asked Felicity.

"Two per car," the guy working the ride said, securing their safety bar.

"Don't worry! I've got Ashley!" Felicity shouted.

Mary-Kate looked at her sister, and Ashley waved, mouthing, *"Good luck!"* As the ride lurched forward, Mary-Kate gripped the bar in front of her. This was going to be one scary ride.

Romantic violin music filled the air as their car entered the tunnel. On both sides were caricatures of famous couples throughout the ages: Romeo and Juliet, Antony and Cleopatra, Sandy and Danny from *Grease*. A bunch of animated hearts danced all around them, swirling and disappearing, making Mary-Kate dizzy.

"This is too funny," Trevor said, as he looked around. "Do you think anyone finds this romantic?"

Mary-Kate gulped. Up ahead she could see the silhouettes of Cooper and Claudia as they gave each other a smooch.

"Apparently *they* do," she said, earning a laugh from Trevor. Mary-Kate gazed at him. She would so love to be able to kiss Trevor like that.

The ride moved through a heart-shaped door and around a bend into a dark cavern. Mary-Kate's pulse raced. This had to be the section Felicity was talking about. And she had to admit, it was perfect. She could barely even see Trevor, which meant she couldn't look at him and chicken out. Plus if he laughed, she wouldn't be able to see that either.

Okay, what do I say? she thought, trying to ignore the sound of her heart pounding. *"Trevor, we've known each other a long time . . ."* No. *Too serious. How about, "Hey, Trev! Guess what!? I'm totally in love with you!"*

Oh, God, this is suicide.

She could hear Trevor breathing next to her. His leg brushed against hers.

Just do it! she told herself as the ride continued to move. *This is your chance!*

"Trevor?" she said, her voice cracking. "There's something I have to ask you."

"Yeah? What's that?" Trevor asked.

"I . . . well . . . do you think you—"

Suddenly the entire tunnel was illuminated, bathing the car in bright pink light. There was Trevor, in full view, and Mary-Kate's mouth snapped shut. The moment was over. She'd missed it. She had wasted too much time deciding how to start.

"Do I think I what?" Trevor asked.

Mary-Kate panicked. What should she say? How could she get out of this? Then she noticed her camera dangling from the strap around her wrist. Perfect!

"I wanted to take a picture of you!" Mary-Kate announced, hyper with nervousness.

She pulled the camera off her wrist, but it slipped and went over the side. Mary-Kate leaned out to grab it, but suddenly there was a loud, grinding, crunching sound, and sparks popped and sizzled from the track. The ride slammed to a stop and Mary-Kate pitched forward, her stomach mashing into the safety bar.

"Oh . . . ow!" Mary-Kate said, leaning back and holding her stomach. "What just happened?"

Trevor angled himself out of his seat to look over her side, where the camera had disappeared.

"Mary-Kate, I hate to tell you this, but I think you just killed the Tunnel of Love," he said. And then he laughed like he'd never laughed before.

Mary***Kate invites Claude18 to Instant Message!

Claude18: hey . . . how're u doing?

Mary***Kate: I can never show my face again.

Claude18: it wasn't that bad. . . .

Mary***Kate: Carlos got me on film being dragged out of the Tunnel of Love by a security guard!!!

Claude18: ok. that is kind of bad. . . .

Mary***Kate: It's gonna be in the yearbook next year!!!

Claude18: look at it this way—at least they decided not 2 arrest u!

Mary***Kate: I think Trevor is still laughing out there somewhere.

Claude18: so the plan didn't work. we'll think of something else.

Mary***Kate: OK. We'll do that tomorrow. For now I just want 2 go 2 bed and hide under the covers.

Claude18: oh! and don't answer the phone! I heard a local news crew is going to do a story on "Terror in the Tunnel of Love."

Mary***Kate: That's it. I'm moving to Mexico.

CHAPTER EIGHT

Ashley threw her arms into the air and cheered as Buzzkill finished their first song. The open-air arena was sold out, and every inch of the place was packed with crazed fans. The crowd around her screamed and clapped. The noise was deafening.

"This is awesome!" she shouted to David, over the wail of the guitar as the band started their next song. Logan O'Neill, the lead singer, jumped up onto one of the amps to sing, and everyone screamed even louder.

"I know! I'm so glad you came!" David shouted back.

"Me, too!" Ashley replied. "They're amazing!"

Together they sang along to the next song, "You Know You Love Me." Ashley laughed when she saw a bunch of girls at the end of their row get out into the aisle and dance around like maniacs.

"So you're having a good time?" David asked, leaning toward her so he didn't have to shout so loudly.

"Yes!" Ashley replied. "The best!"

She was so glad she had agreed to go out with David again. She really was having fun. Maybe there was no attraction between them, but that didn't mean she and David couldn't be friends. And he hadn't tried to hold her hand or anything all night long. Everything was turning out for the best.

"Hey!" David shouted.

"What?" Ashley asked, turning to face him.

Suddenly David grabbed her and planted a long kiss right on her mouth. Ashley never even had a chance to close her eyes. It was awkward and dry, and he clutched her arms a little bit too hard. All Ashley could do was stand there, wishing it would end already.

"Wow," David said when he finally released her. "I was just caught up in the moment."

"Uh . . . yeah," Ashley said. *What moment? Did I miss something?* she wondered. Buzzkill was playing one of her favorite songs now, but she couldn't even catch the beat. She just felt too guilty and awkward and icky. Meanwhile David was beaming as if he'd just experienced the most amazing kiss of his life.

"So, Ashley," David said. "I was wondering . . . do you want to go to the prom? With me?"

Omigosh! What am I going to do? Ashley wondered, her mind reeling. *Just say no! Say no, thank you. Tell him you don't like him that way!*

But David looked so hopeful, she couldn't crush him.

"Um . . . maybe?" she said, biting her lip. "I just . . . can I think about it?"

David's smile faltered for a moment but quickly

came back. "Sure. No problem. Just . . . let me know."

"Thanks. And thanks for asking," Ashley said, glad he hadn't asked for more of an explanation. She tried to get back into the concert, but she knew she was going to be uncomfortable for the rest of the night. Sooner or later she would have to turn David down. He just wasn't the prom date of her dreams.

But who was?

"It couldn't have been that bad," Mary-Kate said as she and Ashley walked toward the school gym on Saturday morning to work on prom decorations.

"It was awful," Ashley said. "I had no idea what to say. And then the good-night kiss was even worse! I already wasn't attracted to him. What am I going to do?"

"Why don't you just *tell* David you're not attracted to him?" Mary-Kate asked as she yanked open the door. "Why didn't you just say no to the invite?"

"It was too hard!" Ashley said. "He really likes me. He's practically picking out our wedding cake."

"You've only been out on two dates," Mary-Kate said, stepping into the gym, which was already packed with kids working on prom decorations. "Just . . . let him down easy."

"I don't know how," Ashley said. "I guess I have to."

"All right. Enough guy talk," Mary-Kate said, dropping her keys into her bag and glancing around. "What do we need to work on?"

"We need about a million silver and gold stars to hang from the balloon ribbons," Ashley said, leading Mary-Kate to some tables and chairs in a corner. "What do you think?"

"Sounds good to me," Mary-Kate said, picking up a star stencil. "I can't make too much of a mess with scissors and a pattern, right?"

Ashley laughed, and she and Mary-Kate pulled out chairs. Ashley outlined the stars on silver paper, then handed them to Mary-Kate to cut out.

"I feel like we're back in kindergarten," Mary-Kate said. "Remember Ms. Kelso's arts and crafts?"

"How could I forget? You were at the nurse's office every day for eating paste," Ashley said.

Mary-Kate's hands dropped to the table. "Um, hello? That was you, my friend."

"Was not!" Ashley countered. "*You* were the paste-eater!"

"You are so delusional!" Mary-Kate laughed.

"Whatever, Elmer's-lover," Ashley teased.

"Delusional girl!" Mary-Kate said.

"Um, excuse me. Hate to break up what sounds like a major argument. . . ."

Mary-Kate looked up to find Billy Suskin hovering at the end of their table. They had been lab partners in chemistry all year.

"Ha ha," Mary-Kate said. "What's up, Billy?"

"Well, actually, I know this is sort of out of nowhere,

Mary-Kate, but I was wondering, if you're not going with someone already, would you go to the prom with me?" Billy rambled.

Mary-Kate's face flushed. She looked at Ashley, who shrugged as if to say, "He *is* cute." But it didn't matter how cute Billy Suskin was. Mary-Kate already had a date to the prom—one she wanted to keep.

"Actually, I'm going with Trevor Reynolds," Mary-Kate said. "But thanks for asking."

"Oh, no problem," Billy said, forcing a smile. "I'll . . . uh . . . I'll see you there."

Mary-Kate sighed and looked at her sister as Billy strolled away. "Now that's how you let someone down easy," she said.

"Very funny, paste-eater," Ashley said with a smirk.

They got back to work, but moments later Hunter slipped into the seat next to Ashley's.

"Nice stars," he said, looking over the pile they made.

"Thanks," Ashley said. "How long have you been here?"

"About an hour," Hunter replied. "I was working on the plane when I saw you come in. I was wondering if you'd like to go out again tonight. I want to check out that classic film festival at the old theater downtown."

Mary-Kate watched as Ashley's whole face brightened. Instinctively she knew her sister was about to say yes, so she did the only thing she could think of to stop her: She kicked her ankle under the table.

"Ow!" Ashley glared at Mary-Kate, who tilted her head, hoping for a twin-mind-reading moment. Suddenly Ashley's eyes widened, and her face paled.

"Oh, actually I already have plans for tonight," Ashley told Hunter. "Maybe we can do something tomorrow?"

"Sure. I'm free," Hunter said. "I'll give you a call."

After he'd moved on to inspect the next table of workers, Ashley's head hit her arms. "I can't believe I almost forgot I have a date with Joe tonight." She lifted her chin to look at Mary-Kate. "Thanks for the save."

"What are sisters for other than to be your personal date book?" Mary-Kate joked.

"You know, you are just full of good ones today," Ashley shot back with a smile.

Suddenly Ashley's cell phone beeped. She pulled it out of her bag and checked the screen. The message icon was flashing. When she hit the button to see who called, David's and Carlos's names filled the screen.

Mary-Kate laughed. "Just let me know if you need any more help keeping them straight," she said.

Later that evening Mary-Kate was surfing the Web when the phone rang. She grabbed it quickly, expecting a call from Trevor.

"Hello?"

"May I speak to Ashley, please?" a guy's voice asked.

Mary-Kate rolled her eyes as she got up from her desk. "Who's calling?"

"This is David . . . again."

Mary-Kate hit the MUTE button on the cordless and walked into Ashley's room. Her sister was standing in front of the mirror finishing off her mascara, already dressed for her date with Joe. She had chosen her favorite red sundress and strappy sandals, topped off with a pair of chandelier earrings.

Mary-Kate whistled. "You look fab," she said.

"Thanks," Ashley replied with a smile. "Who's on the phone?"

"Oh, just David . . . again," Mary-Kate said. "And while you were in the shower, Hunter left you a message about tomorrow, and Carlos called. He sounded *desperate* to talk to you."

Ashley groaned and tipped her head back. "He's calling about my speech," she said. "I still haven't worked on it." She took a deep breath and stared at her reflection. "But it's okay. I know what I want to say . . . mostly."

"Well, do you want to talk to David or not? He's still holding," Mary-Kate said.

"Can you tell him you just missed me?" Ashley asked, biting her lip. "Joe will be here any minute."

Mary-Kate walked out into the hall and took her finger off the MUTE button. "David? I'm sorry, but you just missed her. She's out for the night."

"Oh, okay," David said, sounding disappointed. "Just tell her I called?"

"No problem," Mary-Kate said before hanging up.

She leaned into the doorway to Ashley's room. "So what's the deal?" she asked. "Are you going to call him?"

"I will . . . I guess," Ashley said with a pained look. "I just don't want to hurt his feelings."

"Well, what if he finds out you're going out with Hunter and Joe? That'll probably hurt his feelings," Mary-Kate said. "I'm worried about you, Ashley. You're not used to all this guy juggling."

"Tell me about it," Ashley said. "It's totally exhausting!"

Mary-Kate laughed, and a horn honked on the street down below. They both ran to the window to see Joe stepping out of his gleaming red convertible with a huge bouquet of roses.

"Flowers?" Mary-Kate said, raising her eyebrows.

"Wow," Ashley said. "On a scale of one to ten, he just went from an eight to a nine."

She gave Mary-Kate a quick hug and ran out, bubbling over with excitement. Mary-Kate watched as her sister walked down to the car with Joe, who opened the door for her and everything.

"Unreal," she said to herself. "I can't even tell *one* guy I like him, let alone two or three."

She took a deep breath and stood up straight. It was about time she took a hint from Ashley. She had to go out and get what she wanted.

Mary-Kate was going to tell Trevor how she felt about him, and she was going to do it tonight!

Mary***Kate invites Claude18 and Felicity_girl to Instant Message!

Mary***Kate: I've decided. I'm going 2
do it tonight. Now tell me something
2 keep me from chickening out.

Felicity_girl: confused! do what 2nite?

Claude18: obviously she's talking about
trevor, f!

Felicity_girl: hey! not a mind reader
over here!

Mary***Kate: Can we focus? I have 2
leave in a few minutes to meet him.

Claude18: ok, look, no way is trevor
going 2 reject u! He LUVS U!!!

Mary***Kate: LOVES me or loves me as a
friend?

Claude18: come on! we've all seen the
way he is around u! u r, like, the
focus of his universe.

Mary***Kate: REALLY???

Felicity_girl: and look at it this way—
if he DOES reject u at least the
school year is over.

Claude18: FELICITY!

Mary***Kate: Gee. That's helpful.

Felicity_girl: just telling it like it
is. now go get 'im, tiger!

CHAPTER NINE

Ashley walked out of the Olde Tyme photo booth at the yearly town carnival and removed the old-fashioned bonnet from her hair.

"That was so cool," she said.

Joe untied the bandanna from around his neck and smiled. "I've always wanted to do this," he said, taking off the cowboy hat and hanging it on a free hook in the dressing room. "When I heard this carnival had one of these booths, I knew we had to find it."

"Well, thanks for including me," Ashley said, un-Velcro-ing the satiny dress she had put on over her own clothes. She was flattered that Joe had chosen to share something he'd "always wanted to do" with her. She walked out to the front of the booth, and the man behind the counter handed her the black-and-white photograph he had taken of them.

"This is awesome," Joe said, looking at the picture over her shoulder. He paid for two copies. "Okay, what next? We did something I wanted to do. Now we do whatever you want to do."

Ashley smiled and tipped her head back to look at him. "I'm thinking . . . cotton candy," she said.

"I've never had it," Joe replied.

Ashley's jaw dropped. "You're kidding!"

"There's a first time for everything," Joe said.

Ashley practically dragged him to the snack bar in the center of the bustling carnival. Bells dinged from game booths, kids screamed on the rides, and music blared from speakers placed all around. Ashley ordered two huge cones of cotton candy and handed one to Joe. He hesitated, so she took a big bite of her own, letting the sugar melt in her mouth.

"Mmm. So good," she said. "Go for it."

Joe took a bite and made an odd face but then gradually started to smile.

"Wow. What have I been missing?" he said.

"Aren't you glad you went out with me?" Ashley asked jokingly.

"So glad," he said, causing Ashley's pulse to quicken.

"What now?" Ashley asked, floating somewhere above the carnival in a happy daze.

"Well, I hate to brag, but I'm an expert at the bowling game," he said. "I think you deserve to go home with a huge teddy bear tonight."

"Sounds fair," Ashley said. "I mean, I *did* introduce you to cotton candy."

Joe smiled, then reached out and took her hand in his. Ashley's heart fluttered around as if it had wings.

She had never felt like this with David *or* Hunter. Could it be that in the middle of this sudden dating marathon she had actually found "The One"?

Mary-Kate got a chill when she stepped out of her SUV at the beach and closed the door. And it wasn't because the air was cold. Trevor walked around the front of the car with their coffees and headed for the beach, totally clueless about the fact that Mary-Kate was about to change their entire relationship.

She pulled a blanket out of the backseat and followed him down to the sand. Once the blanket was smoothed out, they sat down next to each other, and Trevor passed her the decaf latte.

Trevor sighed and looked up at the stars. "This was a good idea," he said. "The ocean always helps me chill out."

"I know," Mary-Kate replied.

They had been coming to this beach together since they were kids. They had come here after Trevor thought he failed his bio final in tenth grade. They had come here after he took second place in an art competition that everyone agreed he should have won. Mary-Kate knew Trevor was happiest here.

"Hey! Remember that class trip to collect seashells in second grade?" Trevor said suddenly.

Mary-Kate laughed at the memory. "Are you kidding? That was the first time I beat you up."

"You did not beat me up," Trevor protested. "That wrestling match was a draw. Ask anyone!"

"How did that start again?" Mary-Kate asked, narrowing her eyes as she tried to remember.

"You took that crab shell I found," Trevor said.

"Oh, right! You mean the crab shell *I* found."

"Please! I so had that first!" Trevor replied, getting up on his knees.

"Whatever. The important thing is, I won the wrestling match," Mary-Kate said, lifting her shoulders.

She loved this so much. What would happen if she told him how she felt? Would this all change? Mary-Kate squirmed at the thought. She felt as if she were about to jump off a cliff.

"That's it. I want a rematch," Trevor said, clapping his hands together.

"What?" Mary-Kate said, blinking. "I'm not going to wrestle you!" Here she was about to tell him she was in love with him, and he wanted to go back to second grade?

"What are you, scared?" Trevor teased her.

Mary-Kate narrowed her eyes. She could never back down from a challenge, no matter how many somersaults her heart was doing. "Yeah! For *you*!" she shot back.

"Gimme a break. I can take you right now."

"You cannot!"

"Can so! I've been drinking my milk," Trevor joked.

"Please! You've been drinking coffee," Mary-Kate replied.

"Ah, but there's milk *in* the coffee," Trevor said, putting his cup aside. "You ready?"

"Bring it on," Mary-Kate said, sitting up.

Suddenly Trevor lunged at her, tackling her back into the cool sand. Mary-Kate screeched and fought back, pushing his shoulders until he tumbled backward. They rolled over and over toward the water. Mary-Kate got sand in her hair, in her mouth, and down her shirt, but she barely noticed. She was laughing too hard to care.

"Ah! No hair-pulling!" Mary-Kate shouted, feeling his fingers in her curls.

"No kicking!" Trevor shouted back.

"Ow! Ow! I give!" Mary-Kate said, laughing as he practically twisted her into a ball.

"Winner and still champion!" Trevor called out, releasing her.

They both fell back into the sand, laughing and clutching their stomachs. Gradually they quieted down and caught their breath. Suddenly Mary-Kate could feel Trevor staring at the side of her face. She turned to look at him, and he was only inches away from her. Before she could even take a breath, Trevor had reached over, put a hand on her cheek, and kissed her right on the lips.

Mary-Kate's heart soared as she kissed him back. They sat up, their lips never parting, and her eyes fluttered closed. She couldn't believe this was happening.

Trevor had made the first move. *He* was kissing *her*! All Mary-Kate's dreams had come true.

Then suddenly he pulled away. His hands covered his mouth, and he looked at her, wide-eyed.

"Oh, my God. What are we doing?" he said.

"I don't—"

"No! I'm so sorry." Trevor scrambled to his feet. "I just got—carried away, I guess. That was so stupid."

Okay, not what you want to hear from the love of your life after your first kiss, Mary-Kate thought, reeling.

"We should go," Trevor said. "Let's . . . just go."

And then he tore up the beach, never once looking back.

"I had an incredible time," Joe told Ashley as he walked her to her door that night. She clutched her huge teddy bear under one arm, her Olde Tyme photo stuffed under its shirt.

"So did I," Ashley said giddily. She had never had such a perfect first date in her life.

"I hope we can do it again." He took her free hand.

"Absolutely," Ashley said, tipping her head back.

Joe smiled and leaned forward, touching his lips to hers. His kiss blew away every other kiss she'd ever experienced. Her heart felt as if it wouldn't slow down for days.

"Wow," she said automatically when he pulled away. Then she flushed, embarrassed.

"Yeah. Wow," Joe responded, instantly making her feel better.

"So I'll definitely call you," Ashley said.

"I'll call you first," he replied.

Ashley sighed happily as she opened the door, thinking about what an amazing prom date Joe Laudadia would be.

Walking on air, Ashley placed her bear in the center of her bed, then turned to look for a frame for the photo. That was when her gaze landed on her desk, and her moment of total happiness came crashing down around her.

Her notes for her speech were sitting in the center of her desk, where she had left them to remind herself to get to work. There was practically nothing there—just a few lines of vague ideas and the words CARPE DIEM! in huge capital letters. Who was she kidding? At this rate she was going to have nothing to say at graduation.

So much for lying down and going over her date moment by moment. At least for tonight.

Ashley changed into a pair of sweatpants and turned on her computer. She noticed that she had two unread e-mail messages from Carlos. She sighed, the guilt settling in even further.

She had been too busy having fun and going out on dates. Well, no more. It was work time. By this time tomorrow she was going to have something to tell Carlos. No matter how late she had to stay up to write.

Felicity_girl invites Mary***Kate to Instant Message!

Felicity_girl: well??? what happened???

Mary***Kate: I didn't tell him.

Felicity_girl: u didn't? y!?

Mary***Kate: Well, he kissed me before
I could.

Felicity_girl: WHAT!?!?!? HE DID!?!?!
YAY!!!

Mary***Kate: Not so "YAY." He freaked
and bailed.

Felicity_girl: u r kidding?! Ugh! Boys!
well, was the kiss good?

Mary***Kate: Who cares!? The point is,
he freaked and bailed.

Felicity_girl: yeah. but was it good???

Mary***Kate: Felicity! Ur not hearing
me here!

Felicity_girl: WAS IT GOOOOOD???

Mary***Kate: Yeah. OK. It was really
good. It was actually amazing.
sigh

CHAPTER TEN

So in conclusion I would just like to say to my fellow graduates, get out there and live your dreams," Ashley read with a huge smile. *"Carpe diem!"*

She threw her arms into the air as her grand finale and looked at her sister, who was lying on her bed. Mary-Kate slowly raised her eyebrows and blinked as if she were just waking up from a nap.

"Well? What do you think?" Ashley asked, clutching the page that held her speech.

"Oh. That's it?" Mary-Kate asked.

"Yes, that's it," Ashley said, frustrated. "You didn't like it?"

"No! It was . . . great," Mary-Kate said, sitting up.

Ashley sighed. That was not exactly the reaction she'd been hoping for. Ashley had been up all night working on this speech. Or, well, for an extra hour at least.

"I'm sorry," Mary-Kate said finally. "I'm just not in the best mood."

Ashley's heart went out to her sister. She had heard

the whole Trevor story over breakfast that morning. Poor Mary-Kate was walking around with a broken heart, and here Ashley was hoping her sister would get excited over a silly speech. And she knew that this draft wasn't even her best work.

"Don't worry about it," Ashley said, crumpling the paper in her hand. "It's just my first try. Maybe I should find an inspiring poem or something. Maybe that would be more effective than an original speech."

"I like the *carpe diem,* though," Mary-Kate said, attempting a smile. She pulled one of Ashley's throw pillows onto her lap and hugged it to her. "It's very inspirational."

"Thanks. I'm definitely keeping that," Ashley said. "But maybe I'll just shove one fist into the air instead of both arms, ya think?" She demonstrated for thrusting an arm up like a cheerleader.

"Absolutely," Mary-Kate said.

Ashley sat down on the bed next to her sister and wrapped an arm around Mary-Kate's shoulders. "Okay, you are just too depressing," she joked, hoping for another smile. "Is there anything I can do? Want to go to the mall and vent your emotions with a little retail therapy? It's good for the soul—"

"But bad for the wallet," Mary-Kate finished, smiling. "Thanks anyway, but believe it or not, I'm supposed to meet up with Trevor in a little while. We're going to work on the ba—I mean, the new tradition."

"What is this new-tradition thing anyway?" Ashley asked, narrowing her eyes.

"Sorry. Trevor and I swore we'd keep it a secret," Mary-Kate told her, standing and smoothing her khaki shorts. "I could tell you, but then I'd have to kill you," she added, arching one eyebrow.

"At least you still have your sense of humor," Ashley said, whacking her with a pillow. "Well, good luck. I'm going to work on the speech."

"Good luck to you too then," Mary-Kate said. "We're both going to need it."

Ashley picked up a pillow, but Mary-Kate ducked out of the room before it could hit her. It bounced off the doorjamb and hit the floor. Ashley laughed and headed for her bookshelf to pull out a few poetry volumes. She was going to figure out this speech today if it was the last thing she did.

Mary-Kate hunched over the Ping-Pong table in Trevor's basement, using a pencil to stencil out the number *2004* onto white fabric. They were using the table as their arts-and-crafts space, and it was covered with fabric, paints, scissors, pencils, and glue.

She glanced at her watch for the tenth time in five minutes, nervously wondering when Trevor was going to get back. He had been at the dry cleaners picking up the banner when Mary-Kate had arrived and his dad had let her in. Mary-Kate was half dreading his return.

What was he going to say to her after last night's kiss?

The door at the top of the stairs opened and closed. Mary-Kate felt nauseated. She so wanted him to take back what he'd said the night before—that it was all a mistake. She just wanted him to hug her and tell her he had been replaying the kiss all night, the way she had. Trevor clomped down the creaky staircase with the banner rolled up over one shoulder. Mary-Kate's heart swelled in her chest.

"Hey," he said.

"Hey," she replied. *Say something. Something normal,* she told herself. "How does it look?" she asked finally.

"Unbelievable," Trevor said. "I'll open it up on the floor."

"Wait! We just had it cleaned!" Mary-Kate said.

"I vacuumed this morning," Trevor said with a smile. He tapped his right temple with one finger. "Smarts," he joked.

Okay. At least they were bantering. That was still normal. But someone had to mention the kiss. They couldn't just ignore it, could they?

"Ha-ha," Mary-Kate managed to say. "Let's see it."

Trevor dropped the roll at one end of the room and unfurled the banner until it stretched out a good ten feet. Mary-Kate stepped up in front of it and smiled, even though her emotions were all over the place. The banner looked brand new. All the dust and wrinkles were gone, and now that the dark green background was clean, the colorful dates popped out even more.

"Wow," she said.

"Yeah. It's a masterpiece," Trevor said.

"Where are we going to put our year?" Mary-Kate asked, kneeling next to him.

"I was thinking right about here," he said. He leaned past her to point out an empty spot below *1973* and next to *1981.*

Suddenly Mary-Kate couldn't find her voice. Trevor's arm had brushed her knee and his left cheek was inches from hers. She felt she was about to burst. *This is as good a time as any,* she thought. *Tell him you* wanted *him to kiss you on the beach. Tell him you want to kiss him again.*

"Listen, Mary-Kate, about last night . . ." Trevor said before she could begin. He sat back and looked at her, his eyes apologetic. "I don't know what happened. I must have been under the influence of some alien mind warp or something. I mean, I can't believe I actually kissed you," he added with a laugh.

Mary-Kate felt as if she had been slapped. "What's that supposed to mean?" she asked, standing up. "No one would ever kiss me without mind control?"

Trevor stood up quickly. "No! That's not what I meant. It's just . . . we're friends. Friends don't . . . do that kind of thing. I don't know what got into me."

Mary-Kate stared at him for a moment, wishing she could read his mind. Was he saying he hadn't wanted to kiss her at all? That he had imagined she was some-one else or something?

"Look, all I'm saying is, we don't think of each other that way, right?" Trevor said. "You don't think of me that way, and I don't think of you that way. We're just *friends*."

Mary-Kate swallowed hard. All the daydreams she had been having about Trevor and the prom swirled through her mind: Trevor looking handsome in his tux, having pictures taken with him, holding hands with him, sharing a kiss with him in the middle of the dance floor. Suddenly she realized she had been a fool to imagine any of it. Those things were never going to happen. And if she went to the prom with him, she knew she would just be thinking about those day-dreams, agonizing over the fact that she was so close to them but that they weren't going to come true.

Her senior prom would be sheer torture.

"Trevor, I think maybe we shouldn't go to the prom together," Mary-Kate said shakily. She just wasn't sure she could do it. She wasn't sure she could hang with him at the prom like a best bud when she wanted so much more.

"What? Really?" Trevor asked.

"Well, Billy Suskin asked me, and I kind of said yes," Mary-Kate fibbed. "He's really nice and every-thing—"

"I understand," Trevor said automatically. "It's cool.

We were just going as friends anyway, so if you have a shot at a real date, I get it."

Mary-Kate's heart hurt. She wished he would stop saying *just* and *friends* in the same sentence.

"Good. Thanks for being cool about it."

"No problem," Trevor replied. "So let's get back to work."

"Sure."

Mary-Kate walked back to the Ping-Pong table, swallowing back tears. All she really wanted to do was go home, but she didn't want to be a big baby. She was just going to have to make it through this afternoon. Then she could find Ashley and cry on her sister's shoulder all she wanted.

"Thanks for coming to the beach with me," Ashley said to Hunter, leaning back on her striped towel. "I just couldn't imagine spending such a nice day in a movie theater."

"That's cool," Hunter replied, sitting down next to her. "We'll just have to go to the classic movie fest on our next date."

Ashley smiled, but a little swell of guilt rose inside her. She liked Hunter and wouldn't have minded going out on another date with him, but after Joe, no one else could measure up. Could she really keep playing the field when a guy like Joe was out there?

"It looks like you weren't the only one with the

beach idea today," Hunter said, glancing around. "It's as if everyone from school has come out to worship the sun."

Ashley lifted her sunglasses from her eyes and squinted as she looked down the beach. Sean and Danielle, who'd really seemed to hit if off after she bought him at the auction, were splashing around at the edge of the water. And Ian Taffe and Connor Scott were throwing a Frisbee around behind them. Ashley deflated a bit when she saw them. They were two of David's best friends.

"Wow. Maybe the movie was a better idea," Ashley said under her breath.

"What?" Hunter asked.

"Oh, nothing," Ashley said. She put her dark glasses back on, then grabbed her wide-brimmed sun hat and yanked it down over her eyes.

"You sure cover yourself up a lot for a person who wants to be out in the sun," Hunter said with a laugh as he lay down on his back.

Ashley's gaze darted everywhere. If David was here somewhere, she wanted to see him before he saw her.

"Hey, Dave! Over here!"

Ashley looked up. Sure enough David Ryan was walking down from the boardwalk toward his friends, carrying three sodas. Panicking, Ashley yanked her extra towel out of her bag, wrapped it around herself, and pulled the hem right up under her sunglasses.

"What're you doing?" Hunter asked.

"Do you have any idea how damaging the sun is to our skin?" Ashley asked, watching David from behind her glasses. He and his friends walked off toward a line of beach chairs well down the shore. Ashley loosened her grip on the towel with a sigh. At least they were sitting a safe distance away.

"Come on," Hunter said, standing up and offering his hands. "We're going into the water."

"Why?" Ashley asked.

"Because I think you have heatstroke," he joked.

Ashley took his hands and followed him to the water, turning her head away from David and his friends. She was pretty sure he wouldn't be able to recognize her from that distance, but better safe than sorry.

Hunter dove right into the waves, but Ashley waded in slowly. The water wasn't exactly warm.

"Come on!" Hunter said, waving an arm at her. "It's great once you get wet."

"I don't know," Ashley said. "I don't want to get my hair all tangly."

"Come on, Ash! Live a little!" Hunter said with a grin.

Ashley glanced over her shoulder to see if David had spotted her. That was when she saw something that made her heart plummet. Joe Laudadia jogged toward her along the shoreline. He hadn't spotted her yet, but he would any second. This was no good. Ashley had just talked to him that morning to set up a second date. If he saw her out with Hunter, he might call it off. Ashley looked around for an escape, but there was nothing she could do. She held her breath and dove into the water.

It was freezing! Every inch of her skin was covered in goose bumps, and her lungs were stunned. But she stayed under as long as she possibly could, hoping Joe would be gone when she came up for air.

Suddenly she felt a hand clasp her upper arm, and she was pulled up out of the water.

"Are you okay?" Hunter asked.

"Yeah! Yeah! I'm fine," Ashley said, clearing her eyes and looking around. Joe had passed them by and was still jogging, his back to them now. Ashley let out a sigh of relief.

"You stayed under so long, I thought you were in trouble," Hunter said.

"I'm okay, really," Ashley told him. "I was just . . . getting used to the water."

"Oh. I thought you didn't want to get your hair wet," Hunter said, his brow furrowed.

"Oh . . . yeah," Ashley said, shoving her tangled mane behind her shoulders. "But I was *so* hot, I just had to jump in!"

"Speaking of jumping in," Hunter said. "There's something I've been wanting to ask you, Ashley. Would you go to the prom with me?"

Ashley was so taken off guard, she almost dove

under again. First David and now this? Didn't anyone have a prom date yet? She liked Hunter, but she *really* wanted to go with Joe. Unfortunately he was the only one who hadn't asked her yet.

Ugh! When did this get so difficult? Ashley thought.

"Ashley?" Hunter prompted as a wave swelled by.

"Is there any way we can talk about this later?" Ashley asked. "I'm just not in prom mode right now, you know?"

Hunter looked concerned. "Maybe you *should* get out of the sun. You're looking a little faint."

"Yeah. Good idea," Ashley said. "Maybe we can still catch that movie."

Hunter brightened at the idea. "But that's not a 'no,' right?"

"No. It's not a 'no,'" Ashley replied. "Let's say it's a 'maybe.' Is that okay?"

"Sure," Hunter said.

Relieved, Ashley started back toward the shoreline. At least if they were sitting in a dark, quiet theater, they wouldn't be able to talk about the prom anymore. It would buy her some time to figure out what to do.

And I definitely need to figure it out, Ashley thought. *As soon as possible.*

Mary***Kate invites Claude18 to Instant Message!

Mary***Kate: Do u think Billy Suskin
    will still go 2 the prom with me?

Claude18: i thought u were going with
    Trevor!!!

Mary***Kate: Apparently he couldn't
    care less about me.

Claude18: no way!!! Not tru!!!

Mary***Kate: I don't want 2 talk about
    Trevor right now. About Billy . . .

Claude18: He's a great guy. not a thing
    wrong with him.

Mary***Kate: Except . . .

Claude18: except what?

Mary***Kate: Except he's not Trevor. :(

CHAPTER ELEVEN

The entire senior class gathered on the football field Monday morning for graduation practice. Chairs were set up for the graduates, facing a small stage near the end zone. Everyone was standing in groups, talking about the upcoming prom. Mary-Kate wove through the crowd of people, looking for Billy Suskin. She had to talk to him before he had a chance to ask someone else to the prom. Mary-Kate wasn't sure she could take another disappointment.

Sunday had been torturous. After the talk about the kiss and the prom, she and Trevor had barely said two words to each other all afternoon. At this point Mary-Kate wasn't sure their friendship was ever going to be the same.

She spotted Billy and his friends near the front of the crowd. She made a beeline for them and tapped Billy on the shoulder. He smiled when he saw her.

"Hi," Mary-Kate said. "Can you talk?"

"Sure," Billy replied. He followed her a few feet off, his expression interested.

"I was just wondering if your offer still stands," Mary-Kate said. "For the prom?"

"Yeah!" Billy said, lighting up. "Definitely. But I thought you were going with Trevor."

"That sort of fell through," Mary-Kate said. She glanced up and spotted Trevor on the other side of the field, his eyes trained on her and Billy. The moment she looked at him, he looked away and walked over to Cooper and some other guys. He didn't even smile or wave. Mary-Kate's stomach turned.

"Oh, well, that's great," Billy said, then laughed. "For me, I guess. I'd love to go with you, Mary-Kate."

Billy was so excited that Mary-Kate's awful feelings were quickly erased. She could have done a lot worse. Even if it wouldn't be the ultimate romantic night, it could still be fun. Right?

Ashley sat in her chair on the stage during graduation practice, her palms sweating. Carlos was just finishing up his salutatorian speech, and it was *good*. It was better than good—it was poetic. She couldn't believe she had come here unprepared. It was so unlike her. But after spending the whole day with Hunter and then chatting on the phone with Joe half the night, she hadn't had any energy left to work on her speech.

Everyone applauded when Carlos was finished. Then Principal DiPaolo stepped to the podium, and Ashley stopped breathing.

"Thank you, Carlos," the principal said into the microphone. "It is my pleasure to introduce to you the valedictorian of the Class of 2004, Ashley Olsen!"

Somehow Ashley got out of her chair. The class cheered as she walked shakily to the podium. Her mind was blank. She couldn't even remember a word of the draft she had recited for Mary-Kate the morning before.

Ashley stepped up behind the microphone and adjusted its height, stalling for time. She looked out at the sea of expectant faces looking up at her. There was only one thing she could think to do. She thrust her fist into the air and shouted, *"Carpe diem!"*

Everyone exploded into cheers and laughter. Ashley grinned, and took her seat again. Carlos patted her on the shoulder as he laughed, but Principal DiPaolo did not look so amused. Ashley glanced away guiltily.

Mrs. Purcell, the class adviser, got up to run though the procedure for handing out diplomas. While she spoke, Mr. DiPaolo walked up behind Ashley and leaned down. Her pulse raced nervously.

"Very funny, Ms. Olsen," he said quietly. "But I expect you to have something appropriate prepared by Friday."

"I will," Ashley said with a gulp. "Don't worry. I will."

Ashley rushed to the door when the bell rang that evening, psyched for her second date with Joe. He was standing there, looking gorgeous, holding out a single white lily. Could this guy be any more perfect?

"Thank you," Ashley said, twirling the stem between her fingers.

"You look beautiful," Joe said, holding out a hand.

Ashley grinned as she took it, and they walked together down the front path to his car.

"So what are we doing tonight?" she asked.

"It's a surprise," Joe said. "I hope you like surprises."

"I *love* surprises," Ashley said.

"Good. There's someone I want you to meet," Joe said. "Someone really special to me . . ."

Joe opened the car door, and Ashley was about to sit down when a furry creature started yapping and growling at her from the front seat. Ashley jumped back as Joe reached in and picked up the little animal.

"Shh, Cream Puff," he said. "It's just Ash-wee. I told you about Ash-wee, wemember?"

Baby talk? Joe was talking *baby talk*? "Cream Puff?" Ashley said, taking a step back as the little thing lunged at her.

"She's my poodle. My poodle-woodle-doodle," Joe said, puckering his lips at the dog. "I thought it was about time my two favor-wite girls met. Isn't she the cutest little puppy wuppy in the world?"

"Um . . . yeah. She's . . . cute," Ashley said. She reached out to pet the dog, but it snapped its teeth at her hand. Ashley yelped and pulled her fingers back.

"Oh, calm down, my wittle girl," Joe said to the dog. "You're just a wittle threatened, aren't you? Aren't you?"

he said, holding the dog up to his face. "What if I give you a big fat kiss? Will that make you feel all better?"

To Ashley's horror, Joe kissed the dog right on its snout. The dog reached out with its tiny pink tongue and licked Joe all over his lips. To make matters worse, Joe appeared to be loving it.

This was not happening. That mouth had kissed *her* a few nights ago! Had he kissed his dog before taking her out? Had that little tongue smooched Joe's lips before *he* smooched Ashley? She was reeling from the fact that cooler-than-cool Joe Laudadia was actually a baby-talking freak, and now she had to deal with canine kisses?

"Give her a kiss, Ashley," Joe said, holding the dog toward her. "You know you wanna!"

"Um . . . no thanks," Ashley said, her mind already searching for a way out. She couldn't believe the hottest guy in her class was poodle-obsessed.

"Come on! Just one wittle-bittle kiss!" Joe prodded, pushing the dog at her.

"No, really!" she said, taking another step back. "Actually, I . . . just remembered that I have to . . . uh . . . work on my speech! Yes! Mr. DiPaolo was really mad today and I should really get to work."

"Are you sure?" Joe said, his face falling as the dog yapped at her. "I wanted to ask you about the prom."

The prom! Ashley thought. *Just this morning I wanted to go with Joe more than anything. But now . . . Ugh! Would he bring Cream Puff along?*

"Can we talk about that later? I really have to go," Ashley said, starting toward her house. "I mean, I'll—"

She stopped herself short. She was *not* going to call Joe Laudadia. Not this week, not ever.

"I'll see you at school," she said, smiling sweetly before running back into the house. She didn't want to be mean, but, whoa! This guy was crazy! She slammed the door behind her, taking a deep breath.

So much for the perfect silver-screen prom date. But at least she had two more offers waiting in the wings. Ashley knew she had to call David and Hunter and give them answers about the prom, but just thinking about it exhausted her. She needed some distraction ASAP.

Trudging upstairs, Ashley decided that this would be the perfect time to work on her speech. She changed into sweats, flipped on her computer, and sat down.

"Okay, here goes," she said aloud. Then she typed in her greeting:

Principal DiPaolo, members of the faculty and staff, students, parents, and fellow graduates . . .

An hour later that was all she had. Her mind was a total blank. What could she talk about that hadn't been talked about in every graduation speech ever given?

"I'm going to get booed off the stage," Ashley said to herself, head in her hands.

The phone rang, and she lunged for it, eager for an escape from her mind.

"Hello?" she said.

"Hi, is Ashley there, please?" an unfamiliar voice asked.

"This is Ashley," she said.

"Oh, hi! This is Todd. Todd Parker."

Why was Todd calling her out of the blue?

"Hi, Todd," she said. "What's up?"

"Well, I was just wondering . . . do you have a date for the prom yet?" he asked.

Ashley's stomach turned as she thought about David, Hunter, and Joe. "No, actually."

"I was wondering if you'd like to go with me," Todd said.

Ashley closed her eyes. This was getting out of hand. "What about Kylie?"

"Well, that didn't work out. She's going with Matt Schwartz," Todd said. "So . . . what do you think?"

Ashley took a deep breath. She'd never thought Todd would be calling to ask her to the prom, and it was definitely tempting. But what about David and Hunter?

"Ashley?" Todd asked. "Are you there?"

"Sorry," Ashley said. "Can I think about it, Todd? I'm just a little surprised. . . ."

"Sure. Not a problem," Todd said quickly. "Give me a call when you know."

"Okay. And thanks for asking," Ashley said.

"No problem. Bye, Ashley."

"Bye," she said.

Ashley hung up the phone, blowing out a sigh. So many guys and only one prom. What was a girl to do?

DavidRyan invites AshleyO to Instant Message!

DavidRyan: Yo, Ashley! What's shakin'?

AshleyO: Hi, David! Actually kind of
  busy . . .

DavidRyan: Oh. So have you heard the
  new Buzzkill single?

AshleyO: Um . . . no. I—

<HUNTER> invites AshleyO to Instant
  Message!

<HUNTER>: Hey, Ashley! What's up?

AshleyO: Oh! Hey . . . Hunter . . . I—

#22Todd#22 invites AshleyO to Instant
  Message!

#22Todd#22: Ashley! Ur online!

AshleyO: Todd???

#22Todd#22: That's me, baby!

AshleyO: Oh. Hey. Kind of busy right—

JoLaudad invites AshleyO to Instant
  Message!

JoLaudad: Ashley! Cream Puff wants 2
  say hi!

AshleyO: JOE!?

JouLadad: Joe AND Cream Puff!!!

<HUNTER>: Ashley? Ya there?

DavidRyan: Ashley? Did u get booted?

#22Todd#22: Ash?

AshleyO: Gotta go!!! Byeeeeee!!!

CHAPTER TWELVE

I still can't believe I won the Class Spirit award," Mary-Kate said, beaming over her plaque at the senior awards banquet.

"Please. You've done more for this class than any other ten people combined," Ashley said.

"But don't they usually give it to the cheerleading captain or something?" Mary-Kate asked.

"Yeah. Just another reason for Kristi Carlton to hate you," Ashley joked. They both looked across the banquet hall at Kristi, who'd had a sour expression on her face ever since Mary-Kate's name was called.

"At least DiPaolo smiled when he gave you your award," Ashley continued. "He's still mad at me about graduation practice the other day."

"Forget Mr. DiPaolo. Your speech is going to be great," Mary-Kate said, rubbing her sister's back.

"You think?" Ashley asked.

"I *know*," Mary-Kate replied, earning a smile from her sister.

"And now that all the awards have been given out,

I'd like to call up Mary-Kate Olsen, senior class president, to announce the senior class gift," Principal DiPaolo said. "Mary-Kate?"

Mary-Kate stepped up to the microphone to address the class members and their parents, realizing with a pang that this would be one of the last times she would get to speak to them this way. She took a deep breath and dove in.

"This year's senior class gift, paid for by the many fund-raising efforts of the class over the last year, is a new set of picnic tables and benches for the quad," she announced. "We think it's an even more perfect gift now that we have our new quad centerpiece," Mary-Kate continued. "The new tables will give Crusty the Cow the beautiful home she so obviously deserves. Thank you!"

The crowd laughed and clapped, and Mary-Kate stepped down from the stage, her duties for the night now complete. She walked to the dessert table in one corner, ready to reward herself with a chocolate fix. She noticed that Trevor was hovering at the end of the table, his plate loaded down with cookies and cake.

Mary-Kate immediately froze up with uncertainty. She had barely spoken to Trevor since Sunday, but there would be no avoiding it now.

"Hey," he said flatly when he saw her.

"Hey," she replied, grabbing a plate and napkin. He didn't say anything else, so she busied herself with choosing a dessert.

This was so wrong. Trevor was her best friend. Normally he'd be congratulating her on her award, or they would be joking about the lame food or the weird muumuu-type dress Ms. Cordial was wearing.

"So . . ." Trevor said finally. "Guess I'd better get back to my table."

Then he turned and walked away before Mary-Kate could even come up with an answer. She watched his back as he went. Would things ever be okay between her and Trevor again?

"I got you a brownie," Mary-Kate said, looking sullen as she returned to her table.

"Thanks," Ashley replied as her sister sat down. "What's wrong?"

"Nothing . . . just Trevor, as usual," Mary-Kate said, attempting a smile.

Mr. DiPaolo approached the table before Ashley could get her sister to elaborate. "Mary-Kate, may I speak to you for a moment, please?" the principal asked. "I want to go over the graduation ceremony with you."

"Sure," Mary-Kate said, standing again.

Ashley took a bite of her brownie, scanning the room. Her parents were across the room chatting with Mr. Smith, her English teacher. Felicity, Claudia, and Cooper were talking with their own parents. Ashley was about to get up and join her parents when she saw David heading toward her from the dessert table.

Her body temperature immediately skyrocketed. She still hadn't talked to him about the prom, and she wasn't sure how to tell him no. A teacher moved out of the way, and she saw that Hunter was with David.

Hunter and David? They weren't close friends. Suddenly Ashley's stomach took a nosedive. Neither boy looked very happy. Was it possible they had found out she had said "maybe" to both their prom invites? Then she saw that Todd and Joe were walking behind them as well! All four of them together!

Ashley wasn't about to wait and find out what they wanted from her. In a panic, she stood up and practically ran for the bathroom. She was checking over her shoulder when she slammed right into someone— hard.

"Oof!"

Carlos hit the ground, his ever-present yearbook camera flying from his hands.

"Omigosh! I'm so sorry!" Ashley said.

The second he was on his feet again, she tried to get around him, but Carlos stepped in front of her.

"Hey, Ashley!" he said. "Can we talk for a sec?"

"Um . . . not right now, Carlos," Ashley said, slipping around him. "I'll call you later!"

There were about a dozen girls standing in a group near the bathroom, gabbing and blocking her way.

"Excuse me," Ashley said, turning sideways to try

to slip between a girl's back and the wall. "Can I just get through, please?"

No one heard her. *Just run! Just head for the door and run!* she thought. *Hide in the car!*

She turned around and was about to do just that when Hunter stepped right in front of her. Ashley swallowed a lump in her throat as she looked into his hard green eyes. Then David, Joe, and Todd stepped up next to him. Ashley felt as if she was facing a college admissions board all over again.

"Uh . . . hi?" she said.

"Ashley, funny thing," Hunter began, crossing his arms over his chest. "I was telling Joe all about this great girl I was hoping to go to the prom with, and he was telling me all about this great girl *he* was hoping to go to the prom with, and you'll never guess what happened next."

"You went for cake?" Ashley attempted.

"No. They found out they were talking about the same girl," David said. "And then I overheard them and it turns out the girl *I* asked to the prom has the same name, too."

"And so does the girl *I* asked," Todd added.

"What a coincidence," Ashley said, hoping for some kind of sign that they weren't going to kill her.

"So, any idea who this girl is?" Hunter asked.

"Okay, in my defense, I never said yes to any of you," Ashley said.

"But you never said no either," David said.

Ashley couldn't argue with that.

"So, Ashley, who's it gonna be?" Todd asked, raising his chin. "Which one of us are you going with?"

Ashley's stomach dropped. "You want me to decide right now?" she asked.

"I'd like to know before it's too late to ask someone else," Hunter said.

Ashley took a deep breath. As much as she liked certain things about each guy, at that moment she didn't much like any of them. And even if she did like one of them enough to go to the prom with him, she wasn't sure she was up to rejecting three guys at once.

"You know what, guys? Thanks for asking, but I think I'll go to the prom on my own," Ashley said, almost unable to believe what she was doing. "I'm sorry for all the confusion."

All four guys widened their eyes. Feeling very independent and very dateless at the same time, Ashley turned and walked away. That would teach them never to corner a girl that way.

From four maybe-dates to none in less than twenty seconds, Ashley thought, half triumphant, half disappointed. *It has to be a record.*

Felicity_girl invites AshleyO to Instant Message!

Felicity_girl: hey there, chica!

AshleyO: Hi.

Felicity_girl: whoa. u r so depressed even your IM is lame.

AshleyO: Thanks.

Felicity_girl: what is wrong!!??

AshleyO: I'm prom dateless.

Felicity_girl: there has 2 b someone out there! Get one of our sophomore lackeys to hook u up with an older brother!

AshleyO: Eh.

Felicity_girl: come on! i hear that bobby kid has a brother who plays football at stanford. a stanford man!!!

AshleyO: I don't know. I'm tired of getting 2 know new guys. I need a break.

Felicity_girl: so what r u going 2 do? the prom is on friday!!!

AshleyO: I know. I'll think of something. . . .

CHAPTER THIRTEEN

I can't believe they're green gowns," Felicity said with a grimace as she stepped to the front of the cap-and-gown line on Wednesday morning. "This color flatters no one."

"It's one of our school colors," Mary-Kate said. "Just be glad it's not sunshine yellow."

"That's my sister. Always looking on the bright side," Ashley said, patting Mary-Kate on the back.

"Speaking of bright sides, did you figure out what to do about the prom?" Claudia asked, trying to fit her cap's elastic headband on over her newly red hair.

"Yes," Ashley told them, stepping away from the line. "I have decided to go to the prom alone."

"That is a very brave and cool decision," Felicity said, slipping an arm around Ashley's shoulders. "You are truly a woman of the twenty-first century."

"Thank you," Ashley said with a smile. "You're right. It's going to be cool. Who are you going with, Felicity?"

"Actually Joe called last night and asked me," Felicity said, wincing. "You don't mind, do you?"

"Not at all," Ashley said. "Just *don't* kiss him."

"What? Why?" Felicity asked.

"Trust me," Ashley said. "You'll thank me later."

She turned around and found herself face-to-face with Carlos once again. Instantly Ashley went into panic mode. She still didn't have a speech for graduation!

"Hey, Carlos," she said quickly. "I know you want to talk, but—"

"Oh, no!" Carlos said, stepping in front of her as she tried to get away. "You are not ditching me this time. I've been trying to pin you down for days!"

Tell me about it, Ashley thought, shooting a helpless look at her friends. "All right! I admit it!" Ashley exploded, her nerves finally fraying. "I have no speech! I am speech-less! I have less than nothing to say!"

The entire roomful of seniors fell silent at her outburst. Even Carlos looked a little disturbed.

"Ooookay," he said. "We can figure that out later, but I didn't want to talk to you about your speech."

"Really?" Ashley asked, confused.

"Really. Actually I was just going to ask you to the prom," Carlos said. "I'm sure you already have a date, but I promised myself back in September that I would ask you out before graduation, and now there's only about forty-eight hours left so . . ." He smiled, embarrassed. "Hey, you only live once, right?"

Ashley grinned, surprised. All this time all Carlos had wanted to do was ask her out? That was so sweet!

"So would you like to go with me?" he asked.

"I'd love to go to the prom with you, Carlos," Ashley replied. "Thanks for asking."

"Okay! Mary-Kate and Billy, get together!"

Mary-Kate smiled awkwardly at Billy as she stepped toward him to pose for the camera. She was wearing her strapless blue prom dress, and her hair was piled on top of her head in carefree tendrils. Billy looked handsome in his tux and had brought a beautiful orchid corsage for Mary-Kate's wrist. They looked like the perfect prom couple. Unfortunately Mary-Kate was having a hard time getting into the spirit of things.

"Sorry. My dad's a little bit snap-happy when it comes to big occasions," she said.

"I don't mind," Billy told her with a smile. "Did I tell you that you look beautiful?"

"Yeah," Mary-Kate said, her smile widening. "But I don't mind your saying it again."

He slipped an arm around her and turned toward the camera. Ashley, Carlos, and Mary-Kate's mother looked on as her dad took a few shots. Mary-Kate tried to relax, but she was having a hard time. Billy was being very sweet, but she couldn't stop thinking about Trevor, and about how much more fun this whole thing would be if he were there.

"Now, Mary-Kate and Ashley get together," their father instructed.

Ashley walked over in her slim black halter dress and took Mary-Kate's hand.

"You miss him, don't you?" Ashley asked under her breath.

"Like you wouldn't believe," Mary-Kate said. "I mean, he's my best friend. He should be here even if he's not my date."

"I know," Ashley said, squeezing her hand. "But it's prom night. You have to relax and have a little fun. We only get one of these, you know."

As the camera snapped away, Mary-Kate looked at Billy who was laughing and talking with Carlos. He really did seem like a great guy. It was time to enjoy the moment.

"*Carpe diem*, right?" Mary-Kate said with a laugh.

"Finally! Somebody gets it!" Ashley replied.

"You're a great dancer!" Ashley shouted at Carlos over the pounding music.

"Thanks! So are you!" he replied before executing a little spin.

Ashley was so giddy, she lifted her arms and twirled, the strobe lights blinking all around her. Everyone in the class was dancing and laughing. The prom was a huge success.

Not only that but Carlos was turning out to be the date she had always dreamed of. He looked downright gorgeous in his tux, he was constantly getting her punch, asking her if she wanted to sit, and chatting up her friends. Who knew Carlos Bernal would be such a catch?

Suddenly the hip-hop song died away, and a slow tune started up. Ashley stopped moving and looked at Carlos. It was the first slow dance of the night.

"You up for it?" Carlos asked with a smile, holding out his arms.

"Definitely," Ashley replied.

She moved into his arms, and together they started to sway to the music. As Carlos held her, Ashley suddenly got chills all up and down her spine. She looked into his eyes and noticed for the first time how dark brown and beautiful they were. Why had she never noticed them before?

Carlos looked into Ashley's eyes, and she felt a thrill of attraction. Unbelievable. Maybe this was going to be a romantic night after all!

Mary-Kate hung out by the door with Claudia, sipping her punch and taking a break from the dance floor. The disco ball in the center of the room sprinkled stars over everything, and the music felt as if it were being pumped from inside her own heart.

This was it. Her last high school dance. She had to admit, it was beautiful. Ashley and Carlos were dancing right next to Kristi and Hunter, who had apparently snapped each other up as last-minute dates.

Every once in a while Kristi would glance over at Mary-Kate, clearly wondering why she hadn't come with Trevor. Mary-Kate thought it was kind of funny. Maybe she hadn't gotten to attend the prom with Trevor, but at least he hadn't been stuck with Kristi.

Mary-Kate looked over at Billy, who was talking with some friends a few feet away. He caught her eye and smiled. Mary-Kate smiled back. She really was glad he had asked her to the prom.

"Omigosh. Look who just walked in!" Claudia cried.

Mary-Kate glanced at the door, and her heart lost all control. Trevor Reynolds stood there, tux and all, looking around the room. He looked so amazing, Mary-Kate had trouble catching her breath. "I can't believe he came," she said.

At that moment Trevor spotted her and smiled slightly. He walked right over to her.

"Hey," he said.

"Hey," she replied.

"May I have this dance?" he asked.

Mary-Kate nodded. Her mouth was too dry to speak. Trevor led her to the center of the dance floor and slipped his arms around her waist. Mary-Kate linked her hands behind his neck.

"Mary-Kate, I want to apologize," Trevor said.

"Me, too," Mary-Kate said. "I hate fighting with you."

"What were we even fighting about?"

"I don't know," she said.

Trevor smiled, and Mary-Kate looked away. She watched the couples swirling around the dance floor, looked at the lights dancing against the stars that hung from the balloon ribbons all over the room. This was it. This was the moment she had been hoping for.

"Trevor? There's something I have to tell you," she said, looking up at him. "I do know why we were fighting."

"Yeah?" he said, raising his eyebrows.

"I was mad at you because after you kissed me, you said it was a mistake and . . . I didn't think it was a mistake." Mary-Kate stopped dancing, and Trevor looked at her, perplexed. She took a deep breath. "Trevor, I like you. I mean, I like you as more than a friend. I was afraid to tell you because I didn't want to kill our friendship, but I'm also afraid not to take the chance because . . . because I think we could be really amazing together."

Mary-Kate looked up at him, and Trevor blinked a few times. She was dying from the suspense.

"Well?" she said. "Say something. Anything."

Trevor ran a hand along the back of his neck and Mary-Kate knew he was about to let her down easy. It was torture.

"Mary-Kate," he said, "I've had a crush on you since sixth grade."

Mary-Kate blinked. "What?"

"Yeah," Trevor said with a laugh. He reached out and cupped her cheek with one hand.

"I don't believe it!" Mary-Kate said.

"Me neither!" Trevor replied, grinning. "I only said that kiss was a mistake because I thought *you* only liked *me* as a friend. Well, that and I thought you were going to deck me."

Mary-Kate laughed, relief and joy rushing through her. Trevor liked her! He liked her as more than a friend! She moved back into his arms and leaned her head on his shoulder. Mary-Kate had never been so happy in her life. Her romantic prom fantasy had come true!

"May I cut in?"

Mary-Kate and Trevor looked up to find Billy standing beside them. It hurt to let Trevor go—this could have been the most romantic night of their lives—but Billy *was* Mary-Kate's date.

"I'll see you later?" Trevor asked.

"Yeah," she said. "See ya."

She smiled at Billy as they danced together, resolving to focus on him for the rest of the night, but she knew the second she got home she would be calling Trevor to figure out what it all meant. She glanced over at the door and saw Trevor watching her. They smiled at each other one more time, and then he stepped through the doorway and was gone.

AshleyO invites Mary***Kate, Felicity_girl, Claude18, Cooperman and Trevor86 to Instant Message!

AshleyO: It's graduation day! Whoo-hoo!!!

Felicity_girl: Whooo-hooo!!!

Claude18: Yee-ha!!!

Trevor86: Dude. We're like, adults.

Cooperman: no more teachers, no more books . . .

Mary***Kate: LOL. Well, Cooper's not an adult, anyway.

Felicity_girl: Ash, ur speech ready??

AshleyO: SO ready!

Mary***Kate: She was up all night. Major bags under her eyes. ;)

AshleyO: MK!!!!!! I do not have eye bags!

Claude18: well, i can't wait. carpe diem!

Felicity_girl: OMG! Stop saying that, people!

Mary***Kate: Carpe diem!

Trevor86: Carpe diem!!!

Felicity_girl: NOOOOOOO!!! STOP!!!!!

AshleyO: LOL! See u all there! Go, Class of '04!

CHAPTER FOURTEEN

Well, this is it," Mary-Kate said, grasping Ashley's hand. The opening strains of "Pomp and Circumstance," the traditional graduation march, sounded out over the football field. Up ahead the first members of the class started to march down the aisle.

"I can't believe it. I can't believe we're actually graduating," Ashley said with a grin.

They walked down the aisle until they reached the front. Claudia, Felicity, Cooper, and Trevor sat down in the first row. Then Ashley gave Mary-Kate a quick hug and walked up onto the dais to take her seat next to Carlos. Mary-Kate perched on the edge of her chair, her back straight, and tried to solidify every detail in her memory. The blue sky, the ugly green robes, her sister's smiling face.

Once all the graduates were seated and the music had faded away, Principal DiPaolo stepped up to the microphone.

"Welcome, everyone, to the graduation ceremony for the Ocean View High School Class of 2004!"

His announcement was met with major applause and a few hoots and hollers from the audience. Somebody shouted out Joe Laudadia's name at the top of his lungs, and everyone laughed.

"To begin our ceremony we have a special presentation from our class president, Mary-Kate Olsen, who will be assisted by her friend and partner in crime, Trevor Reynolds," Principal DiPaolo said.

"'Partner in crime'? I like it," Trevor whispered as they stood.

The banner was rolled up neatly next to the podium. Mary-Kate stepped over it and adjusted the microphone.

"This year we decided to bring back a tradition that was kept alive by every graduating class between 1959 and 1989," Mary-Kate said, her voice booming over the field. "Trevor and I did some research and found out that these classes had a banner—one that was used each year in the photo of the graduating class. Around 1990 the banner disappeared. Trevor and I found it, restored it, and made a little change in it. We'll show you what we mean."

Trevor lifted the banner and took one end, while Mary-Kate took the other. Together they unfurled it across the stage until it was fully open. Out in the sunlight the various colors and patterns were even brighter and more colorful. But brightest of all was the year *2004*, a swirl of batik colors that had been added just underneath the words *Ocean View High*.

Everyone applauded, and Ashley took Mary-Kate's end of the banner as Mary-Kate stepped back to the microphone.

"As you can see, each graduating class added their own year to the banner," Mary-Kate said. "Trevor and I decided that the *2004* should be the most colorful one possible to represent our diversity and the melding of cultures throughout the world today. This year for the first time since 1989, our graduation picture will be taken with this banner."

Everyone in the stands applauded, and the class even gave Mary-Kate a standing ovation. Her heart full, she turned around and looked at Ashley and Trevor, who were both grinning.

Now *this* was a moment Mary-Kate would definitely remember.

Ashley fidgeted with the page that held her speech as Carlos stepped down from the podium and sat next to her again. She was nervous beyond belief.

"You're going to be fine," Carlos assured her.

"I just wish I had gotten a chance to practice," she said.

"And now, your valedictorian, Ashley Olsen," Principal DiPaolo announced.

"Break a leg!" Carlos whispered.

Ashley stood up to a round of applause and took her place behind the microphone. She scanned the crowd, finding her parents easily, who were waving at her like crazy. Then she looked down at Mary-Kate, who smiled her encouragement.

You can do this, Ashley told herself. *Just read your speech.* She looked down at the page before her and took a deep breath.

"Principal DiPaolo, members of the faculty and staff, students, parents, and members of the Class of 2004," she began. "After today, everything changes."

Ashley paused, looking at the next sentence. Suddenly she realized that she didn't want to read what she had written, even if it *had* taken her all night. She wanted to speak from her heart. And luckily, at that moment, her heart was so full, she knew what to say.

"Everything changes, starting with this," she said. She crumpled up the paper and tossed it over her shoulder. A few people gasped, and a few people laughed. From the corner of her eye Ashley saw Principal DiPaolo hide his face in his hands. "Those of you who know me know that throwing away that speech was a huge risk for me," Ashley continued. "I'm a perfectionist, and I'm cautious, and I don't take chances. At least that used to be me. Not anymore."

Ashley saw Mary-Kate's grin widen and knew she was on the right track.

"Over the past few weeks I've learned that, while hard work is important, while we need to do our best to go where we want to go in life, hard work is not the only thing that matters," Ashley said. "*Living* your life is just as important. Taking chances, having fun, doing something out of character every once in a while—these things shape who we will become just as much as our grades and our school activities do.

"So my message to the Class of 2004, to *all* of you, is get on out there and have some fun, do something wild, take a chance. If you don't, you may never find out what you're capable of. And we're all capable of so much more than we know."

Ashley paused for a moment, looked down at Felicity and shrugged her apology.

"*Carpe diem!*" she shouted, thrusting a fist in the air.

"*Carpe diem!*" the entire class shouted back at her.

Everyone went wild, applauding and jumping up. People in the crowd laughed and cheered, and flashes popped all around her. Ashley looked at Mr. DiPaolo, who was clapping and beaming with pride.

Ashley laughed, gave a little bow, and returned to her seat. She had already moved on. There was a whole new Ashley on the loose, and the world had better be prepared.

"Donna Oberman," Principal DiPaolo announced.

"We're next," Ashley whispered as Donna went up to get her diploma.

"Hello? I'm about to graduate high school. I know the alphabet," Mary-Kate joked.

"Ashley Olsen," Principal DiPaolo said.

Mary-Kate grinned with pride as Ashley accepted her scroll and moved her tassel from one side of her cap to the other.

"Mary-Kate Olsen," the principal announced.

Mary-Kate rolled her shoulders back and stepped up to take her diploma. She shook hands with the principal, took her scroll, and walked down the steps on the far end of the stage. Back on the ground, she took her seat next to Trevor, feeling totally content. It was over. She was a high school graduate.

"I really liked Ashley's speech," Trevor whispered as the line of graduates continued to inch forward. "Especially the part about taking chances."

"Me, too," Mary-Kate replied.

"So, you're still glad you took the chance you did last night?" Trevor asked.

Mary-Kate's heart skipped a beat. "I am," she said. "Are you?"

"Absolutely," Trevor replied.

Mary-Kate looked into his eyes, and they both smiled.

"Miles Zimmerman," Mr. DiPaolo said. And finally, "Jennifer Zucker."

Everyone waited in silence as Jennifer Zucker shook hands with the principal and walked back to her seat. Mary-Kate's heart pounded with excitement.

"And now, ladies and gentlemen, I give you the

graduated Class of 2004!" Principal DiPaolo announced.

Everyone jumped to their feet. Mary-Kate and Trevor ripped off their caps and tossed them into the air, where they joined hundreds of other flying caps, dotting the blue sky with squares of green. Ashley rushed down from the stage and hugged Mary-Kate, then they both turned to hug their other friends—Felicity, Claudia, Cooper, and everyone else around them. They had done it. They had spent four years in high school and lived to tell the tale!

"Come here," Trevor said, sweeping Mary-Kate up in his arms. She laughed as he twirled her around, her feet swinging through the air.

"Put me down!" Mary-Kate shouted when she finally started to grow dizzy.

Her feet touched the ground again, but the world continued to spin. Trevor touched her face with his fingertips, leaned down, and kissed her, right there in the middle of all the mayhem. Now the world was spinning for a whole new reason.

"This is going to be the most amazing summer ever," he said when he pulled away.

Mary-Kate looked up into his eyes and smiled. "I can't wait."

Book 2
Never Say Good-bye

Ashley planned to make the most of these next three months. She saw many beach parties, bonfires, and shopping sprees in her near future.

Of course, all this fun would cost major bucks, which was why they had all lined up summer jobs. Ashley was seriously considering majoring in pre-law at college, and knew her experience at Atwater, Bumble, and Chang—or "A,B,C," as she was starting to think of it—was sure to help.

"Oops, I've gotta go." Mary-Kate suddenly jumped to her feet.

Claudia groaned. "But we just got started with our fashion show!"

"What's the matter, Mary-Kate, got a hot date?" Felicity joked.

Mary-Kate blushed five shades of red. Ashley knew exactly what that meant.

"You *do* have a hot date!" Ashley exclaimed. She got up and gave her sister a big hug. "Where's Trevor taking you?"

Mary-Kate turned even redder, if that was possible. "I'm not sure. Uh, someplace."

Trevor Reynolds had been Mary-Kate's best bud since forever. Everyone but the two of them had known that they were meant to be together as more than friends, though. During senior week, they had finally figured it out, too. Tonight would be their first official date-date.

"Is it a beach date? You want to borrow one of our bikinis?" Claudia asked her. "You've got ten colors to choose from!"

"You are *not* touching my power suit," Ashley teased her sister.

Mary-Kate laughed as she headed for the door. "Thanks, guys, but I'm all set. I think it's a jeans and T-shirt kind of date."

"Have fun!" Felicity called out. "I'll have my cell in case you need advice. You know, like—if he gets a yucky piece of spinach stuck in his teeth, do you say something?"

"If he orders pesto, should you order pesto, too, so

you both have garlic breath when he kisses you later?" Claudia added, wriggling her eyebrows.

Mary-Kate laughed again and disappeared down the hall. Ashley could tell that her sister was beyond excited about this date, although she was trying her best to hide it. Ashley couldn't wait to get the full run-down she got home.

"Ah, the first date," Claudia said with a sigh. "Is that romantic, or what? I so remember every single detail of my first date with Cooper." Cooper Firenz was her longtime boyfriend.

"I plan to have *lots* of first dates this summer," Felicity grinned. "How about you, Ashley?"

"Oh, I'm kind of first-dated-out," Ashley replied. In an effort to be more fun and spontaneous, she had asked all sorts of guys out during senior week. Unfortunately, she had had some problems . . . juggling. They had all found out about each other and gotten mad at her. She was looking forward to taking a major time-out from dating for a while.

"Besides, there's more to life than guys," Ashley pointed out.

"Yeah, *right*," Felicity said, rolling her eyes.

"There is!" Ashley reached into a desk drawer and whipped out a fresh legal pad. She had a huge pile of them, all ready to go for her new job. "Come on, let's make a list. 'Top Ten Things to Do This Summer!'"

Claudia flopped down on Ashley's bed. "Beach!"

she exclaimed. "That should totally be number one."

The phone rang. Ashley picked it up. "Hello?"

"Ashley Olsen, please."

The unfamiliar-sounding male voice made Ashley sit up straighter. "This is Ashley."

"Good afternoon, Ms. Olsen. This is Ed Lindner from Atwater, Bumble, and Chang."

"Oh, hi, Mr. Lindner. What can I do for you?" Ashley said. She crossed her legs, flipped to a new page in her legal pad, and prepared to take notes. Even though her job wasn't starting for a whole week, they were already calling her! *This is too cool!*

"I'm afraid I have some bad news, Ms. Olsen. The partners just announced a new round of budget cuts. I'm afraid we won't be able to hire any interns this summer. That includes you," Mr. Lindner added.

Ashley froze. *Did he just say what I think he said?* she wondered.

"Ms. Olsen?" Mr. Lindner's voice cut into her thoughts. "We're all very sorry about this. We'll keep your résumé on file for next summer, of course."

Ashley managed to thank him and say good-bye before hanging up.

"Ash? What's up?" Felicity asked her worriedly.

"Earth to Ashley?" Claudia said, waving her hand in front of Ashley's face.

Ashley took a deep breath. "I think I just got fired."

Win the Best Party Ever!

ONE LUCKY WINNER
gets to throw a great party for ten friends!

You receive:
- Karaoke machine
- Fragrance
- Purses
- Cosmetics
- Hair Accessories
- CDs
- Videos

PLUS A $250 GIFT CHECK FOR PARTY FOOD AND GOODIES!

Mail to: **MARY-KATE AND ASHLEY GRADUATION SUMMER SWEEPSTAKES!**
c/o HarperEntertainment
Attention: Children's Marketing Department
10 East 53rd Street, New York, NY 10022

No purchase necessary.

Name:

Address:

City: State: Zip:

Phone: Age:

HarperEntertainment
An Imprint of HarperCollinsPublishers
www.harpercollins.com

DUALSTAR
PUBLICATIONS

Mary-Kate and Ashley *Graduation Summer*
Best Party Ever Sweepstakes
OFFICIAL RULES:

1. NO PURCHASE OR PAYMENT NECESSARY TO ENTER OR WIN.

2. How to Enter. To enter, complete the official entry form or hand print your name, address, age and phone number along with the words "Graduation Summer Best Party Ever Sweepstakes" on a 3" x 5" card and mail to: Graduation Summer Best Party Ever Sweepstakes, c/o HarperEntertainment, Attn: Children's Marketing Department, 10 East 53rd Street, New York, NY 10022. Entries must be received no later than November 30, 2004. Enter as often as you wish, but each entry must be mailed separately. One entry per envelope. Partially completed, illegible, or mechanically reproduced entries will not be accepted. Sponsor are not responsible for lost, late, mutilated, illegible, stolen, postage due, incomplete, or misdirected entries. All entries become the property of Dualstar Entertainment Group, LLC, and will not be returned.

3. Eligibility. Sweepstakes open to all legal residents of the United States (excluding Colorado and Rhode Island) who are between the ages of five and fifteen on November 30, 2004 excluding employees and immediate family members of HarperCollins Publishers, Inc., ("HarperCollins"), Parachute Properties and Parachute Press, Inc., and their respective subsidiaries and affiliates, officers, directors, shareholders, employees, agents, attorneys, and other representatives and their immediate families (individually and collectively, "Parachute"), Dualstar Entertainment Group, LLC, and its subsidiaries and affiliates, officers, directors, shareholders, employees, agents, attorneys, and other representatives and their immediate families (individually and collectively, "Dualstar"), and their respective parent companies, affiliates, subsidiaries, advertising, promotion and fulfillment agencies, and the persons with whom each of the above are domiciled. All applicable federal, state and local laws and regulations apply. Offer void where prohibited or restricted by law.

4. Odds of Winning. Odds of winning depend on the total number of entries received. Approximately 300,000 sweepstakes announcements published. All prizes will be awarded. Winner will be randomly drawn on or about December 15, 2004 by HarperCollins, whose decision is final. Potential winner will be notified by mail and will be required to sign and return an affidavit of eligibility and release of liability within 14 days of notification. Prizes won by minors will be awarded to parent or legal guardian who must sign and return all required legal documents. By acceptance of their prize, winner consent to the use of their names, photographs, likeness, and biographical information by HarperCollins, Parachute, Dualstar, and for publicity purposes without further compensation except where prohibited.

5. Grand Prize. One Grand Prize Winner will win one karaoke machine, 10 Mary-Kate and Ashley back-to-school purses containing Mary-Kate and Ashley merchandise (party music CDs, videos, fragrance, cosmetics, hair accessories) and $250 to be used by winner toward the purchase of party goods and food. Approximate combined retail value of prize totals $1000.00.

6. Prize Limitations. All prizes will be awarded. Only one prize will be awarded per individual, family, or household. Prizes are non-transferable and cannot be sold or redeemed for cash. No cash substitute is available. Any federal, state, or local taxes are the responsibility of the winner. Sponsor may substitute prize of equal or greater value, if necessary, due to availability.

7. Additional terms: By participating, entrants agree a) to the official rules and decisions of the judges, which will be final in all respects; and to waive any claim to ambiguity of the official rules and b) to release, discharge, and hold harmless HarperCollins, Warner, Parachute, Dualstar, and their respective parent companies, affiliates, subsidiaries, employees and representatives and advertising, promotion and fulfillment agencies from and against any and all liability or damages associated with acceptance, use, or misuse of any prize received or participation in any Sweepstakes-related activity or participation in this Sweepstakes.

8. Dispute Resolution. Any dispute arising from this Sweepstakes will be determined according to the laws of the State of New York, without reference to its conflict of law principles, and the entrants consent to the personal jurisdiction of the State and Federal courts located in New York County and agree that such courts have exclusive jurisdiction over all such disputes.

9. Winner Information. To obtain the name of the winner, please send your request and a self-addressed stamped envelope (residents of Vermont may omit return postage) to Graduation Summer Best Party Ever Winner, c/o HarperEntertainment, 10 East 53rd Street, New York, NY 10022 by April 1, 2005.

10. Sweepstakes Sponsor: HarperCollins Publishers, Inc.

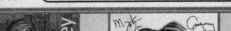

mary-kate olsen   ashley olsen   eugene levy

new york minute

In Theaters May 7th

www.newyorkminutemovie.com